"Faherty writes this era like he was there."

CrimeSpree

HOLLYWOOD IN THE NOIR AGE

Scott Elliott, whose acting career ended with the war, takes on his grimmest case as a private detective in this new novel from multiple-Shamus winner Terence Faherty.

Paddy Maguire, who played a loose game for decades as head of the Hollywood Security detective agency, is dead in an alley — after coming out of retirement to follow a case that should have remained buried in a gangster's lurid past.

As Elliott sets out to even the score, the shadow of an old murder falls across his screenwriter wife Ella, putting their troubled marriage in further jeopardy. They're both about to learn that there is no such thing as a "retired" killer.

D1566381

PRAISE FOR TERENCE FAHERTY:

KILL ME AGAIN

"Alive with the music of 1947, the voices of the era, the smell of the postwar, refreshingly straightforward and evocative . . . easily one of the best of the year. Don't miss it." *Mystery Scene*

COME BACK DEAD
(Shamus Winner)

"I was hooked on the ambience of old Hollywood and an Indiana that doesn't much exist anymore, and on the strength of Faherty's characterizations . . . Elliott makes a tough, principled protagonist in this unique and satisfying series."

Cleveland Plain Dealer

RAISE THE DEVIL

"Faherty's wry humor and laconic style carry the plot through several twists . . . The fun derives from Faherty's blend of real Hollywood history with the fiction necessary for the plot."

Chicago Sun-Times

IN A TEAPOT
(Shamus Nominee)

"The story is engaging from the first paragraph, and Faherty's writing is smooth as sixteen-year-old Scotch. A wonderful mystery from a true master of the PI genre." *CrimeSpree*

PLAY a COLD HAND

Books *by* Terence Faherty

About Scott Elliott

Play a Cold Hand (2017)
Dance in the Dark (2011)
The Hollywood Op (2011)
In a Teapot (2005)
Raise the Devil (2000)
Come Back Dead (1997)
Kill Me Again (1996)

About Owen Keane

Eastward in Eden (2013)
The Confessions of Owen Keane (2005)
Orion Rising (1999)
The Ordained (1997)
Prove the Nameless (1996)
Die Dreaming (1994)
The Lost Keats (1993)
Live to Regret (1992)
Deadstick (1991)

Other

Files of the Star Republic (2017)
Tales of the Star Republic (2016)
The Quiet Woman (2014)

PLAY a COLD HAND

A SCOTT ELLIOTT HOLLYWOOD MYSTERY

TERENCE FAHERTY

PERFECT CRIME BOOKS

Library of Congress Cataloging-in-Publication Data
Faherty, Terence
Play a Cold Hand / Terence Faherty

For Ted Fitzgerald, Ted Hertel Jr., and Gary Warren Niebuhr

CHAPTER ONE

The call came in after midnight, the midnight of May 14, 1974, to be precise. The policeman who'd placed the call, a lieutenant named Ed Sharpe, didn't verify that he'd gotten the right party or even identify himself. He said only, "Alameda and Second. It's Paddy."

I don't remember the drive downtown. The foot of the alley where Sharpe met me was over lit by the carnival lights of two squad cars. They blocked the view of the dozen lookers-on who had gathered in spite of the hour. Dress extras, Paddy would have called them.

Sharpe was, like me, a World War II survivor. He'd been working vice when I'd last run into him. Now he was in homicide. He had the look thin men get at a certain age, the look of an orange rind about two thirds squeezed out. In Sharpe's case, the desiccation was partly an illusion created by the ties he never fully tightened, their big loops making his skinny neck seem even skinnier. His face was similarly diminished in comparison with his big eyes, bloodshot now in the red lights of the black-and-whites.

"Sorry, Scotty," he said and led me in.

Patrick J. Maguire, my onetime boss and mentor, was lying on his back with his feet toward the dead-end of the alley. He was dressed in a too-big suit, making him look like another victim of Sharpe's wasting disease, which he was, though Paddy had once had a big advantage over the cop in girth. The only part of him that retained its old breadth was his Irish face. It looked perfectly peaceful now, as though he'd yet to notice the dark wound in his chest.

On one long wrist, Paddy wore a copper MIA bracelet. I knew it bore the name of my son, William Elliott. On the pavement next to Paddy's thin silver hair was a pearl gray homburg hat. Not a new one, if they were even still making new homburgs in 1974, but one that had been lovingly kept. Without thinking, I bent to pick it up.

"Don't," a voice at my elbow said.

It wasn't Sharpe's voice, though it did belong to a policeman, Captain Walter Grove. Grove was small for a cop and very small for a captain, though he carried himself like a much bigger man. His brown eyes were so dark that it took the full sun or a battery of Klieg lights to make them look anything but black. At that moment, they looked as black as I'd ever seen them.

I would have been expecting Grove if I'd been thinking about anything but Paddy. Grove had been promising me for decades to be on hand when Paddy and I got what was coming to us. Paddy had gotten his, and here was Grove.

"Carrying a firearm, Elliott?" he asked.

"No," Sharpe answered for me, though he hadn't patted me down.

It would have made the moment perfect for Grove if I had been. And if the gun had been fired recently. Paddy murdered and me going down for it would have been Christmas on the Fourth of July for Grove. I started to say as much, but the captain stepped on my line.

"The old man was carrying. Had a snub-nosed thirty-eight in his right-hand coat pocket. He can't have been expecting what he got, though, or the gun would've been in his hand."

I disagreed, silently. On the ground next to Paddy was an unlit cigar, a double corona, its tip almost bitten through. As long as I'd known him, Paddy had gone into action with an unlit cigar in his teeth. He'd been ready for trouble when he'd entered that alley. But someone had been readier still.

"What was he working on, Elliott?"

"He hadn't worked on anything but the crossword puzzle in years," I said.

Grove's answer was to glance down at the man at our feet. It was an argument I couldn't counter. Again, Sharpe spoke on my behalf.

"Nothing you knew about, anyway."

"How about this new Hollywood Security?" Grove asked. "You two working for them?"

"I am," I said, though I was certain Grove was well aware of that. "Paddy never set foot in their offices. And I'd know if he had," I added before Sharpe could issue another disclaimer on my behalf.

Grove summed up my testimony. "So you've no idea what big score Maguire was after."

"How does a 'big score' figure into this?"

Grove's answering laugh contained no merriment whatsoever. As far as I knew, it never had.

"I've been around down-and-outs all my life," he said. "Hollywood's lousy with them. They're always after a big score, something to get them back where they think they used to be, the top of the heap. Most of the time, they're kidding themselves about their old place on the heap. About the big score that's just around the corner, they're always kidding themselves.

"You can make book on it, the old mick was chasing a pot of gold tonight. But the leprechaun beat him to the draw."

That was more philosophy than I'd ever heard from Grove. Just then, I was more interested in nuts and bolts.

"When did it happen?"

My question snapped Grove out of his musings. "We ask the questions, Elliott, we don't answer them." The last half of that line was delivered straight to Sharpe. The next warning was for me alone. "And we investigate murders, not you. You're just a civilian; I don't care what your business card says. And civilian meddlers are a murderer's best friends." He looked down again at Paddy. "Especially the shadier civilians."

The cop who hates private eyes was a movie cliché, but that had never bothered Grove. He signaled to two bit players, the men who were waiting to carry Paddy away. I had a sudden, uninvited memory of a visit to a West Hollywood bungalow way back when I'd started with the original Hollywood Security, Paddy's

Hollywood Security, the company he'd founded in the early forties to protect the movie studio's delicate employees from the sharper corners of reality. It had been my first visit to a murder scene, and an LA cop—Grove's then boss—had held the body in place until Paddy and I arrived.

That now retired detective had tendered the courtesy because he'd wanted something from Paddy, namely information. Grove might have claimed the same motive if I'd asked him why he'd waited for me to arrive, but I wouldn't have believed it. I knew he'd left Paddy on the greasy dirt because he was relishing the moment. And twisting the knife in me.

I almost called him on it, but that would've just sweetened his drink. Instead, I bent down and squeezed Paddy's forearm. Then I told Sharpe to list me as next of kin and left to make some calls.

CHAPTER TWO

Paddy's funeral didn't draw like it would have, once upon a time. He got a few faded stars, though, notably William Powell, over eighty and seldom seen outside of Palm Springs, and Powell's former costar Joan Crawford, who arrived veiled like a sultan's favorite wife. Also Bob Hope, who remembered when Paddy had been a gate guard at Paramount in the thirties. So did the director Billy Wilder, another attendee, who claimed it was Paddy who'd first snuck him onto the Paramount lot.

The priest who led the service at All Souls Chapel hadn't known Paddy that well, which may have been a break for both of them. The gaps in the priest's knowledge had been alternately filled in and papered over by my wife Ella, a screenwriter and former Hollywood publicist. It was hard for me to say, while listening to the priest sum up Paddy's life based on Ella's notes, whether she'd leaned more on her screenwriting or her public relations experience when she'd written them. Paddy came off as a kind of modern-dress Robin Hood, robbing from the rich of greater Hollywood and giving to the poor. That Paddy had died poor himself helped to support the fiction, perhaps. Anyway, no one present demanded equal time.

I referred to Ella just now as my wife. It would have been more honest to say she was my estranged wife. We hadn't been living together for over a year. Not long after our twentieth wedding anniversary, our son Billy had been reported missing in Vietnam. Ella had never really forgiven me for taking on a job while we'd waited for news of Billy, though we'd continued to live under the same roof for a time. When she'd finally been ready to move on, she done it without me. Our daughter Gabrielle, who was now at UCLA, split her time away from the campus between my little place in Malibu and Ella's mountain hideaway.

My son was much on my mind during Paddy's funeral, perhaps because Billy had never gotten a funeral himself. Ella wouldn't hear of it, not even after the American POWs had returned in Operation Homecoming and Billy hadn't been among them. Paddy, Billy's volunteer grandfather, had supported Ella in this. He'd never stopped believing that Billy would show up one day.

Every time I thought of Billy at the funeral, I touched the pocket of my suit coat to make sure I hadn't lost the MIA bracelet Paddy had worn for him. It had been returned with the rest of Paddy's effects when his body had been released. I'd considered burying it with Paddy, which would have given Billy a small piece of a funeral. But I didn't want to make a hard day harder for Ella. For the same reason, I didn't carry the copper band where she could see it.

That was a precaution I'd hardly needed to take. After a few mumbled words, Ella avoided me during the service, leaning on Gabrielle's arm instead. At the Maguire gravesite in Calvary Cemetery—just one row down from Lou Costello's, as Paddy had liked to brag—Ella and Gabby had looked almost like sisters, both slender, Gabby taller and dark, Ella shorter and blond.

After Paddy's coffin had joined that of his wife Peggy, I found myself at the head of an unofficial receiving line, made up of former Hollywood Security clients and even a few ex-employees. Most had a story about Paddy to tell but few had kept in touch with him.

One who had was a short, balding black man named Casper Wheeler. I knew him as the owner of Wheeler House, a hotel in South LA whose Amber Room had been one of the best spots for live jazz in the 1950s. I'd never associated Wheeler and Paddy. When I admitted that, Wheeler shook his head sadly.

"Oh yes, we went way back. I knew his Miss Peggy, too, a fine woman. She was the brains of the outfit, as Paddy always said. I was shocked when I saw him recently. He looked so wasted away. Losing Miss Peggy did that to him. The spark went out in him, that's what I believe, the spark of life that holds a person together. When it's gone, the wind just takes what it wants till there's nothing left."

The last person in line was Gabrielle. Before we were done hugging, she told me her mother was waiting for her in their hired limo, establishing a timetable for our meeting. There were tears in her big eyes, but she didn't offer up any stories about her ersatz grandfather. We'd both had our fill of those for the moment.

"How's the *Mannix* business?" she asked instead, naming a currently popular private eye show. The series' original premise had had an old school PI going to work for a modern, computer-driven detective agency, which reminded Gabrielle of my situation at the reborn Hollywood Security.

"Next time I see Mike Connors," I said, naming *Mannix*'s star. "I'll ask him."

Gabrielle waited me out. She didn't believe in unanswered questions. Or in repeating herself. I often felt sorry for her professors.

"It's fine," I finally said. "The young guys treat me like the interns treated Dr. Gillespie."

"Just don't let them wheel you around in a chair."

I promised I wouldn't. Gabrielle had a different promise in mind.

"You're going to get the guy who murdered him, aren't you, Dad?"

"Given Paddy's history, it could've been a woman."

"You know what I mean."

"I do. And I will."

I didn't add the word try, didn't even think it. This was one promise I wouldn't hedge on.

"It shouldn't have happened," Gabrielle said. Then she said what we all were thinking. "It shouldn't have happened *now*, when Paddy was no threat to anyone."

I thought she was getting philosophical, as Captain Grove had in the alley. For Gabrielle, it would have been more in character, since she was a poet. "Not a beat poet," she'd joked once. "An offbeat one."

I knew we weren't discussing philosophy when she fixed me with a look she'd learned at her mother's knee. The now-hear-this look, I called it.

"That's a clue, Dad. The murder shouldn't have happened in the present, so it must have happened in the past. You'll have to remember that to solve it."

"So now I have to solve a murder *and* a riddle?"

"Dad." Her tone was reproving, but her eyes were now dry. "Take care of yourself. No leading with your right."

"No leading with my right," I said.

CHAPTER THREE

Despite my confident promise to Gabrielle, my investigation into Paddy's murder got exactly nowhere. None of my contacts, some of whom were Paddy's old contacts, had heard anything before his death or anything useful since. The exception was Ed Sharpe, who defied Captain Grove's instructions and passed on the little he knew. Paddy had been shot with a thirty-eight. Paddy's gun, also a thirty-eight, hadn't been fired, maybe not for years. Time of death had been estimated, as there were no witnesses. The best guess was that Paddy had drawn his last breath sometime between eleven and eleven-thirty. His body had been discovered just before midnight by two teens looking for a quiet place to unload the beer they'd been drinking.

After a couple weeks of no success, I took a break from my leave of absence and returned to the "new Hollywood Security," as Grove had dubbed it. Our offices were in Century Tower, one of the high-rise office buildings that were transforming the Los Angeles skyline. We had an entire floor; not the top floor, which would have been ostentatious, but not within walking distance of the sidewalk either.

When I stepped out of the elevator, Paddy was waiting for me. That is to say, his effigy was, the portrait in oils the firm had commissioned. It had been done from a photo that had run in the LA *Times* in 1948, after we'd broken the Ian Kendall murder. That had been a proud moment for Paddy, which first the camera and then the artist had captured. All the details—the rosy, Pat O'Brien jowls, the graying hair that stood at attention in front, the eyes that were a touch harder than the smile—were right except one: the necktie. Paddy had favored ties that were a little louder than the Rose Bowl on New Year's Day. For some reason, the artist had muted this one, making it dull enough for any banker.

The painting should have had a little plaque beneath it that read "our founder," but didn't. Not yet, anyway. Now, if the new management liked, it could add a brass version of Paddy's headstone, complete with name and dates. The painting had acquired one thing since my last visit: a bit of black cloth draped over the top of the frame as a crape.

The right to use Paddy's image had been part of the deal he'd struck with a New York investment group, AMI, when he'd sold them Hollywood Security. There'd been little left to sell by then, except for the name and an almost legendary reputation. But the name and the reputation were almost all that AMI had wanted.

The events that had made a security company in California an attractive investment for New York money men were the murders committed by Charles Manson's "family" in 1969, the brutal killings first of actress Sharon Tate and her four companions and then of executive Leno LaBianca and his wife Rosemary. Overnight, movie stars and the well-heeled in general had begun demanding personal security and lots of it. AMI had initially tried to buy an existing uniformed security company, but those had all been priced like gold claims. So they'd bought out Paddy cheap and whipped up a new Hollywood Security, complete with a "Uniformed Security Unit," something Paddy had never had time for. In Paddy's dictionary, "security" had meant working behind the scenes to defuse a bad situation. You couldn't work unnoticed if you were trailed by a platoon of semipro policemen.

I said earlier that almost all AMI wanted was a name and a reputation. The item I omitted from their shopping list was me, Scott Elliott, a living, breathing souvenir from Hollywood Security's glory days. I'd gone along with the deal because just then I'd needed a reason to get out of bed in the morning. And because the AMI payment would clear up the medical bills Paddy had collected during his wife's last illness.

My office was down a hallway to the right of the Paddy Maguire shrine. It was a nice office, one befitting a star specimen like me. Ironically, I'd never had a space of my own at the old Hollywood Security, if you didn't count the driver's seat of whatever car I happened to be using. This office had a nice view of LA's perpetual haze, broken in the foreground by other buildings and in the background by some foothills of the Santa Monica Mountains, where Ella now resided. The room was furnished in modern, Scandinavian pieces that Ella would have liked and that I liked because they, like the mountain view, reminded me of her.

Vickie, the secretary I shared with the other operatives in the Investigation Unit, stuck her head in to tell me how sorry she was about Paddy.

"I wish I'd known him," she said to break the silence that followed my nodded reply.

Paddy would certainly have enjoyed that meeting, as Vickie looked like Suzanne Pleshette's kid sister. She even shared the actress's basso profundo voice, which she now dropped an extra octave to impart a confidence.

"Mr. McLean asked me to tell him when you came in."

"Tell away," I said.

Hodson McLean was the general manager of Hollywood Security, AMI's man on the scene in Los Angeles. General manager was nowhere near grand enough a title—Paddy had gone by president and he'd never had a third of the employees—but it seemed to suit McLean. He was one of nature's managers, a guy you could have put in charge of anything from a Hamburger Hamlet to Exxon and never sweated an audit. I'd trusted Paddy with my life, but not to pay the electric bill. That had been Peggy Maguire's department. With McLean, I never worried about the lights coming on. How safe my life was in his hands had yet to be determined.

My summons to his office, a corner office with views of the haze in two directions, came right on the heels of Vickie's heads-up. McLean was seated behind his own stretch of Scandinavian hardwood, working away in shirtsleeves. If he'd been wearing sleeve protectors like some old movie accountant, I wouldn't even have blinked. His whole head was as rosy as the cheeks on Paddy's effigy, even his hair, what there was of it. His eyebrows were a shade more golden than the fringe above his ears and very full, his big eyes blue, his nose pug, his mouth given to wry, secret smiles.

He smiled one of those smiles now as he said my first name in greeting. "Scott" often prompted one, since McLean was a Scot himself, a real one, Edinburgh born and raised.

"Thank you again for representing us at the funeral," he said, the burr in his voice ruffling his r's like a soft breeze over the heather. "Have you learned anything?"

I gave him a short, negative report.

"Well, I know you won't give up. Nor would we want you to. Use the firm's resources as you think fit. If I've any criticism of you at all, Scott, it's that you don't lean on the support staff as heavily as you might. I know," he said, countering the objection I hadn't made, "the habits of a lifetime. Just remember that you're not alone in this."

He may have sounded too sentimental to his own ear, because his business side immediately stepped up. "So far, the newspaper stories about Mr. Maguire's death have resounded to our benefit. Proof, if any more were needed, that there's no such thing as bad publicity. We've received a number of calls from new prospects."

He consulted a typed list. "One of those calls concerned you directly. That is, the caller, an Amos Decker, asked for you by name. Heard of him?"

"There's a young screenwriter and director by that name," I said. "One of the bunch the Hollywood old guard is trusting to save their pensions."

"That must be the man. Mr. Decker said he is concerned for his safety, but he wouldn't discuss the nature of the threat with anyone but you. He also wouldn't say who had recommended you. It must have been a satisfied customer, though."

McLean made it sound as though they were legion. I couldn't think of any recent ones for whom I'd done anything more important than coaxing a cat from a tree. Not in the two beats McLean gave me for thinking, anyway.

"I know the timing is bad, Scott, but I'd appreciate it if you would go and see Mr. Decker. Who knows? Maybe a little break from the Maguire investigation will be a positive thing. 'A change of work is as good as a rest,' my granny used to say. Talk to him, find out what the problem is, and then recommend a security system or maybe a period of uniformed monitoring or whatever you think best. If it does turn out to be a job for the Investigation Unit, you can delegate that as well. Sound acceptable?"

"Sounds acceptable," I said.

CHAPTER FOUR

The appointment Vickie made for me with Amos Decker let me sleep in the next morning. Not because it was a particularly late appointment, but because he and I lived in the same neighborhood. And then again, we didn't. Malibu was too big to be a neighborhood. It wasn't formally incorporated as a town, either, but people still referred to it as one, a very long, very narrow town squeezed between Santa Monica Bay and its namesake mountains and bisected by the Pacific Coast Highway, which ran just above the beach. Clinging to the roadway was a strip of houses that started and stopped and widened and narrowed as the topography dictated for a run of over twenty miles.

When Ella and I bought in in the fifties, our cottage had been on a stretch of beach the locals were already calling "the other Malibu," meaning the wrong side of the tracks. Decker's address was in "*the* Malibu," the old Malibu Movie Colony, where the silent movie stars of the 1920s had built their weekend getaways. Since the coming of talkies, those properties had been changing hands steadily. Sometime after the war, the original movie star cottages—never as humble as the word "cottage" suggested—had started to disappear altogether, replaced by bigger and bigger homes on the same modest lots. The result looked like a used car lot for beach houses, one with way too much inventory on hand.

Amos Decker's house, a collection of flat-roofed glass cubes trimmed in cedar, was one of the newer models, but then so was

Decker. The late sixties—a brief, sometimes loving, sometimes violent period—had held the whole country upside down and shaken it, and it had been especially hard on Hollywood. The old studios, what was left of them, had lost millions turning out the kind of movies they'd always turned out, featuring names that had been bankable a few years earlier and now suddenly weren't. In desperation, the studio heads had turned to kids barely out of film school who spoke the new language of the new times. And not just turned to them, but thrown them the keys to the kingdom.

I parked my company car, a Lincoln Continental Mark IV, next to an even newer Cadillac Eldorado convertible whose vanity license plate read "mogul." A young woman in bra and panties lay across the car's big backseat. She was so pale, I would have checked her for a pulse if she hadn't been snoring away like Li'l Abner. As it was, I was tempted to put up the car's top before the sun could get to her.

More bad signs for local real estate values stood on the concrete front porch: a double row of empty champagne bottles. I started to word a joke for whoever answered the door, something about the neighborhood being so nice the milkman delivered Bollinger's. Then I asked myself what the chances were that anyone in the house would be old enough to remember when milk was delivered and gave the effort up.

The person who eventually answered my knock might not have remembered milkmen, but she did remember me. "Mr. Elliott," she said and smiled.

Her name was Polly Hayden, and she was as near to being an established star as it was possible to be in those antiestablishment times. I hadn't heard that she and Decker were an item, which showed how unestablished I'd become. Though she was in her early twenties, Hayden, delicately beautiful, with a waif's big eyes and always short, always tousled blond hair, had so far limited her roles to teenagers, from what I'd seen of her work. Very lost teenagers, usually. At that moment, the lost part looked like typecasting.

She pressed the back of her right hand against one temple. "Amos said he had somebody coming. He didn't say it would be you."

"I'm surprised you remember me," I said.

Hayden and I had met five years earlier, when we'd been members of a doomed expedition, a film crew sent in to shoot a few scenes against the background of the monster rock concert that had all but leveled Avenal, California. Hayden had been one of the actors, and I'd been the crew's entire security staff. Its entirely inadequate security staff. It had been her first movie and very nearly my last.

"I'll never forget Avenal," she said. "I almost ran right back to Pasadena to get my teaching certificate."

"I'm glad you didn't."

She smiled her now famous smile and asked me in. "I'm sorry about the mess," she said. "We had a preview celebration last night for Amos's new movie. But it's always a mess. Amos likes it that way. He finds chaos stimulating."

"Maybe he just likes having someone picking up after him."

The living room was going to require several someones. Discreet someones, too, as the mirror-topped coffee table in the conversation pit was so liberally sprinkled with leftover cocaine it looked like it had been dusted for fingerprints. Not far away stood a refugee from a dentist's office, a missile-shaped tank labeled nitrous oxide.

"Decker's such a good host he even supplies the laughs?"

Hayden's hand went back to her temple. "Laughing gas is supposed to boost creativity, believe it or not. I don't touch that stuff myself. I think it might be dangerous."

Before I could offer a couple of cautionary tales, an interior door flew open and Smokey the Bear came in. Or his stunt double, a big man, shaggy of head and limbs, heavily-bearded, and dressed, like the sleeper in the Cadillac, in underwear only. He descended into the pit and sat down next to the glass-topped table. Then he looked around at the empty seats and blinked.

"Where is everybody?" he demanded.

"Asleep or gone, Bimbo. The party's been over for hours."

"Shit," the man said. He got up and marched out the way he'd come, the room shaking to each flat-footed step.

Hayden said, "Bimbo is a school buddy of Amos's. As near as I can figure, he came out for a visit a year or so ago and decided to stay."

"You just paraphrased the motto of Southern California."

Bimbo's attire having prodded my memory, I told Hayden about the girl in the Caddy.

"Must be Mirabelle. She's supposed to be an earl's daughter or something. I've been wondering what happened to her. Bedrooms were at a premium last night. Private bedrooms couldn't be had."

Hayden sounded like she might be considering another dash to Pasadena. She shook it off. "Maybe you'd better wait out on the balcony, Mr. Elliott. I'll find Amos."

Instead of going off to look for him, she led me out onto the deck, which faced the bay and ran the width of the house. Then she lingered there, admiring the view. It was a view worth lingering over on that very clear morning, as it took in the whole of Santa Monica Bay, from Point Dume to the Palos Verdes Peninsula.

"I'm sorry about Avenal," Hayden said without preamble. "I'm sorry we ran off and left you there. I've always felt bad about leaving you and that boy who died."

We stood thinking about that dead "boy," who'd been the age Hayden was now. Who would always be that age. Her apology solved a mystery for me, or so I thought. I'd been wondering why Amos Decker, a man I'd never met, had asked for me by name. It could have been a client referral, as Hodson McLean believed. But I was now sure that Polly Hayden had done the referring as an overdue compensation for Avenal—or a penance.

"What does Decker need exactly?" I asked. "Besides a live-in cleaning staff."

"I don't know," Hayden said. "Whatever it is, I hope you can help him. He thinks he has the world by the tail, but I think the world has him. Hollywood has him. Amos and all the other geniuses who think they're going to remake this place are getting remade themselves. He doesn't see it."

"Doesn't see what?" a voice behind us asked.

CHAPTER FIVE

The voice belonged to Amos Decker. He wasn't as boyish as his publicity photographs, but probably none of those had been taken before noon with the reflected glare of an entire bay hitting him square in the face. He was dark-haired and bearded like Bimbo, but the beard was trimmed and the hair loosely curled. He wore aviator glasses, tinted enough to make his dark eyes hard to read. The large, full mouth was an easier study. Its downward curve said he wasn't pleased to be the topic of our conversation.

That must have been Hayden's guess, too, because she promptly lied to him. "I was just saying you didn't understand why this view of the bay is called 'the Queen's Necklace.' I was about to ask Mr. Elliott about it. It's something to do with all the lights at night, isn't it? But why Queen's Necklace? Why not St. Monica's? It's her bay."

It looked for a moment like Decker would call her bluff. Then he turned to me and said, "So?"

"Norma Shearer named it," I said. "In 1938, she made a movie called *Marie Antoinette* that retold an old scandal about a diamond necklace the Queen of France may or may not have ordered while the peasants were starving. When Shearer saw the lights of Santa Monica Bay one night after the picture wrapped, they reminded her of the paste necklace MGM had whipped up for the movie. At least, I think the stones were paste. In those days, MGM might have sprung for real diamonds."

Hayden had gotten a little of her color back while I'd rambled. Now she said something about seeing to Mirabelle and hurried off.

Decker watched her go. "Is that Shearer story true?"

"I'd be surprised," I said.

He forced a chuckle or cleared his throat; it was hard to tell which. "Have a seat. The suit and tie weren't necessary, by the way."

I'd guessed that from the open paisley shirt and cutoffs he was wearing.

"Our corporate dress code," I said. I promptly violated that code by taking off my jacket and loosening my tie a la Ed Sharpe.

We sat at a cedar table under a square umbrella that was flapping in the bay breeze like a loose sail. For a time, sitting seemed to be all Decker wanted to do.

Then he said, "Damn noisy gulls. Know any way to get rid of them?"

"Move to Indiana. Of course, they've got crows."

Another chuckle. "Coffee?"

"No, thanks."

"How about a drink? You're the right generation for a martini."

"A Gibson," I corrected, though that was just a martini in sheep's clothing.

"I can send out for the makings."

And we could sit and listen to the umbrella until they came. "A little early for me."

"I thought you detectives were big drinkers."

"Ever since Nick Charles, we've been trying to cut back. You told Hollywood Security you were concerned for your safety."

That got me a third chuckle, a real one this time. "I guess you and I are even on stories that aren't true. I just said that to get you out here. I wasn't sure your boss would let you loose if I told him the truth."

"Which is what?"

"That I want pick your brain. Don't worry, I'm willing to pay whatever your corporate rate is for whatever time I use. Plus a bonus."

"That was all you needed to tell any boss I've ever had."

Decker's earlier bad humor was gone, replaced by an enthusiasm that made him seem boyish, bad lighting or no bad lighting.

"I'm researching a new script, Scotty. Do you mind if I call you Scotty?"

As a matter of fact, I did, Decker being much closer to Gabrielle's age than mine. But a man who couldn't overlook informality in matters of speech or dress or sexual hygiene had no business working in movieland.

"That's fine," I said.

"Is it true you shot it out with the gangster Johnny Remlinger?"

The umbrella flapped with emphasis, and I almost jumped. Remlinger's name still had that effect on me. "Is your script about Remlinger?"

"No, he's just someone I came across while I was researching you. I found out that you used to be an actor, too. I had a friend at Paramount dig *Second Chorus* out of the vault and screen it for me. I couldn't spot you in it."

"You must've been staring at Paulette Goddard's legs. If you're thinking of filming a biography of me, think again. You wouldn't sell enough tickets in my hometown to pay the projectionist."

"It's not a bio, not exactly." Decker paused and licked his heavy lips, which I thought was the windup before the pitch. Then he took another hard left. "Did you see *The Sting*?"

"Yes."

"What did you think of it?"

"They should have made Robert Redford cut his hair. And the ragtime music was all wrong."

That hit a nerve. Decker actually sat up. "Are you kidding? That score's started a Scott Joplin revival."

"A lot of good that did Joplin. He died when Woodrow Wilson was president. And ragtime with him. *The Sting* was set in '36. Nobody outside of a rocking chair was listening to ragtime by then. Duke Ellington's music would have been a better fit. And he'd make better use of a revival."

I said it before I remembered that Ellington, the man who'd composed the soundtrack of my life, was now as dead as Joplin. Cancer had taken him within two weeks of Paddy. May of 1974 wasn't a month I'd happily live through again.

"What music would you pick for a movie set in 1952?" Decker asked.

"A movie about what?"

"A con game. My working title is *The Shuffle*. The con I want to use is the Kansas City Shuffle."

"I think they're already planning a sequel to *The Sting*."

"Of course they are," Decker said. "It made a mint. I'm not interested in imitating that piece of fluff. I want to make the picture it should've been, a tougher, more realistic picture. But I don't mind people thinking mine is an imitation. In fact, I'm counting on that.

"You see, my last two pictures, they were triumphs artistically, but not moneymakers. I'm afraid the same will be true of the one we previewed last night. I was already getting pressured on the budget for that one. But if the bankers think I'm going commercial by cashing in on *The Sting*, they'll be handing me blank checks. Then I'll give them a blockbuster *and* art."

And snow for Christmas, I thought. "Where do I come in?"

"I'm told Hollywood Security ran a Kansas City Shuffle against a Warners producer named Ted Mariutto in 1952. That's what I want to hear about. That's what I want to write about."

I almost changed my mind about sending out for Gibsons. "Who told you that?"

"I'm sorry, Scotty. I promised to protect my source. But she assured me that you were the man to talk to."

I hadn't heard Mariutto's name since his obituary ran in 1970. That obituary had barely mentioned Mariutto's movie producer phase. The writer had been more interested in his earlier career as a racketeer. There'd been a time when no local paper would have dared to mention that. Not because Mariutto was especially tough himself but because he'd been under the protection of Morrie Bender, *the* tough guy, as far as the LA syndicate was concerned. Bender had lived to be ninety and been dangerous every day up to and including his last one.

I'd been wrong about Polly Hayden being the person who had recommended Hollywood Security and me. She'd barely been old enough to sit up in 1952. And whatever her concerns were for Decker, they couldn't have anything to do with this script idea. Mariutto wasn't a threat to anyone now, which made discussing Mariutto's past a safe way for Decker and me to spend a quiet hour on a sunny deck. But I had no desire to do it. So I objected on technical grounds.

"The Mariutto business wasn't that involved. I mean, it was nothing like the plot of the Newman-Redford movie. *The Sting* used a variation on the Big Store con. Those involve a lot of people and a big setup, like the phony betting parlor in the movie. The Kansas City Shuffle is a much simpler con. It's about misdirection, like a shell game. You're just trying to make the mark look at your left hand while you're palming the pea with your right. That wouldn't fill a two-hour movie."

Decker had hung on every word of my lecture but not, as I'd hoped, because he was buying.

"The Mariutto con was more complex than that," he said. "Maybe more complex than you knew."

He might have said more if Polly Hayden hadn't come out just then. "The studio car is here for you, Amos. Did you forget about the postmortem for the preview?"

"Fuck," Decker said, which I took for a yes. To me, he said, "Look, Scotty, you go home, make yourself a pitcher of Gibsons, and try to remember everything you can about Ted Mariutto. We'll meet back here at the same time tomorrow. On second thought, make it after lunch."

CHAPTER SIX

Polly Hayden had rescued the earl's pale daughter as she'd promised. After checking the Eldorado, I backed my Continental around the studio's idling limousine and left the Colony. Not heading west for home, as instructed, but east along the coast highway.

The Continental Mark IV had been selected for the agency's VIPs by Hodson McLean, who'd wanted to project an air of success. It was one policy of the new Hollywood Security that I was totally behind. My leaser had dark red paint, a tan vinyl roof complete with opera windows, a matching tan leather interior, and power everything. I'd only baulked at the car phone McLean had tried to install. I never wanted to be that accessible. The option I most liked was the eight-track quadraphonic stereo, a Ford Corporation exclusive. Once on the highway, I popped in the cartridge containing Duke Ellington's *New Orleans Suite*, and Johnny Hodges' alto sax came through like he was riding along in the backseat.

The exit Johnny and I took was a familiar one, Topanga Canyon Road. That is, the road was familiar. The scenery had been altered beyond recognition by the big fire of the previous year. I'd almost been a party to a forest fire in the canyon in 1964, though in the end that blaze had only claimed an old film. I could still smell the ashes of the '73 fire, even with the windows up, but that might just have been my state of mind. Eventually, I gained the high ground and Mulholland Drive.

I took Mulholland east to the Hollywood Hills and Caverna Drive, where Ella now lived. Seen from Caverna, her house looked like a flat-roofed ranch that was mostly two-car garage. Actually, there was another story, a lower one made possible by the slope of the hill. The upper story had a cantilevered balcony with views of the San Fernando Valley that, at night, had lights enough to make necklaces for all the queens who'd ever lived. The house was an early work of Pierre Koenig, a midcentury modernist. The inside was as spare and rectilinear as the outside, not that I'd seen much of the inside. My information came from Gabrielle, a frequent houseguest. And an impressionable one. She called the house "the nunnery," because of its modest comforts. I knew from long experience that Ella bought furniture for its looks and not its back support. According to Gabby, there weren't even many uncomfortable pieces in the Caverna house and nothing but a bed and a dresser in Ella's own room, which Gabby called "the cell." That room did contain one decoration: the double portrait of the kids we'd commissioned from a moonlighting MGM studio artist, way back when. Gabrielle hadn't mentioned seeing a painting of me, not even one done from an old newspaper photo. That was just as well, given the kind of painters Ella favored. I might have ended up with both ears on the same side of my head.

I had to park diagonally across the short drive to clear the street. Before climbing out, I took off Billy's MIA bracelet and pocketed it. Also my wedding ring. I'd noticed at Paddy's funeral that Ella was no longer wearing hers. It had been a bad day all around.

If I'd left those precautions for the front step, I would have left them too long. Ella opened the door before I could knock. That she hadn't connected the sound of a car with me was conveyed by the way she drew back at the sight of me. I didn't react to that, and my reward was an invitation to come in.

"I'm sorry, Scotty. I should've called you weeks ago. Paddy's murder's been so hard. I was thinking of giving therapy up, not that long ago. Now I don't know if I ever will."

She'd been at work at an older form of therapy— screenwriting—when I'd knocked, or so I guessed from her attire, a sweatshirt over jeans and mismatched socks. Without shoes she was very petite. She was also very thin, I was sad to see. I knew from the way my daughter caught up on her eating when she stayed with me that Ella's aesthetic lifestyle extended to her pantry. Two more clues that she'd been working were the marks on her slightly crooked nose from the reading glasses she must have left on her desk and the state of her hair. It wasn't as blond as Polly Hayden's but it was every bit as short and even more disarrayed—something Ella did with her left hand unconsciously whenever she had a pencil in her right.

"Have you found out anything?"

"No," I said.

I hadn't really talked the case over with Hodson McLean. He wasn't what you'd call a sounding board, unless the subject was an expense account. Ella had been one of the great sounding boards once, on any subject. We sat in her brittle living room and I told her about it, my voice echoing slightly off the all but bare walls and the gleaming maple floor.

"Nothing adds up, not that I even have enough numbers for serious addition. The folks at the Motion Picture Country House told me that Paddy had a visitor a week before he died. A woman, maybe in her fifties, with black hair, which, in the opinion of the only aide who could remember seeing her, was a wig."

As Ella well knew, Paddy hadn't really belonged in the Country House, a retirement facility set up for veterans of the Hollywood studios, actors and production people both. Though he'd once worked in silent films as a baggy pants comic, he fell short of the twenty years of service needed for admission to the home, even after you added in the time he'd spent guarding Paramount's famous gate. He got in through a conspiracy of his old friends, myself included, who had persuaded the home's directors to take into account Paddy's "special services to the film industry."

Those services all involved the original Hollywood Security. Many a big name had had a career saved by Paddy's good offices, even one or two of the Country House's trustees. So winning Paddy his quiet place to die hadn't been that hard a job. Only Paddy hadn't used that quiet place.

"Right after that visit, Paddy started making day trips into the city. No one thought to call me about it, even though they know me, because Paddy told everyone that I'd been in an accident and he was visiting me at Good Samaritan Hospital. Nobody thought to check on that either."

"Where did he get the money for cabs?"

"He had a little spending money. Knowing Paddy, he might have had more squirreled away. Or this mystery woman might have given it to him, if he was working some job for her."

"You weren't able to trace the cabs he used?"

"Tracing the ones he used to get downtown was easy. There's only one cab company in Woodland Hills and only two drivers. Both remembered Paddy. He made four trips in total, always to the same place, Good Samaritan."

"But he wasn't actually visiting anyone there."

"I don't think so. I showed his picture in every ward. With the old-timers, I didn't need a picture; they all knew Paddy. But nobody had seen him inside the place for years."

"So," Ella said, "he was just there to switch cabs."

"Yes. They're always coming and going at Samaritan, but there's no cabstand anymore, so I couldn't ask any regulars about picking Paddy up."

"He wouldn't have used a cabstand if there'd been one."

"No. I spent a day or two bothering cabbies who were delivering fares. And I left fliers at the cab companies and offered a reward. No one's come forward to collect it."

"Paddy probably rewarded his drivers in advance to keep quiet," Ella said.

"Or they heard what happened to him and don't want to get involved. He always arrived back at the Country House on foot, which got the groundskeepers' attention, Paddy not being one for regular exercise. I think he was paying off his cabs where nobody could see a name or number."

"Was he afraid of being tailed?"

"I don't think so. That last precaution wouldn't shake a tail. I think he was trying to make sure his movements couldn't be traced by anyone afterwards. And by anyone, I mean me. You may recommend therapy for me, but I think Paddy was covering his trail because he knew I'd be following it sooner or later."

Ella didn't offer her therapist's name. "If he did that, it can only be because he knew how dangerous that trail was," she said.

I next catalogued the people I'd been to see trying to pick up a trace of that trail. It was a who's who of Los Angeles, with special emphasis on the movie business. Ella's pale blue eyes began searching for something more interesting in the corners of the room. I decided I'd better get to the real purpose of my visit before she remembered the writing she'd left unfinished.

"Hollywood Security's sent me out on something else. Amos Decker called them and asked for me personally. Ever met him?"

"Never when he was sober," Ella said. "He's one of the New Wave kids. The current wave is cocaine, I think."

Ella had a professional's disdain for anyone who wasn't as disciplined as she was. It was tempered by a professional's appreciation for solid work. "His first two pictures were good, *Wild Oats* especially. But too much is coming too quickly to those kids. What did he want?"

"To pick my brains, what there is of them, for a new script he's working on. Is there any chance you wrote down some notes about what Hollywood Security pulled on Ted Mariutto in 1952? Or maybe you did a script proposal based on that that's kicked around the studios and found its way to Decker."

I was curious about Decker's anonymous source, whom he'd called "she." Of the women who'd known about the con, I could only think of two who were still alive. One was Ella.

"You're wasting your time on that?"

Ella's voice was suddenly flat and cold. I saw at once that I'd stepped in quicksand. My taking up a case while Billy was missing had led to our eventual breakup. Ella's therapist had tried to get her past it, had told her that she was suffering from a form of survivor's guilt, blaming herself for going on with her normal life when Billy couldn't and punishing me for beating her to it. And now I was doing it all over again, humoring a spoiled movie brat instead of avenging Paddy.

"No," Ella said, "I never wrote a word about Ted Mariutto. And I wouldn't trust Amos Decker with any idea I cared about. If you're wise, Scotty, you won't trust him either."

CHAPTER SEVEN

The only thing I knew for sure about the Amos Decker business was that I couldn't delegate it. It was Scott Elliott or no one, as far as Decker was concerned. So, after leaving Ella's, I didn't go to Hollywood Security in search of a fall guy. Instead, I made another round of the cab companies and visited an old friend of Paddy's, a retired businesswoman named Mary Jordan, who'd been out of town when I'd made my first pass through the Paddy Maguire who's who. Jordan, who'd run a telephone answering service until it was made obsolete by answering machines, was so shocked by the details of Paddy's death that she actually shed a tear, which shocked me. It was the first I'd ever seen from her, and I'd served as a pallbearer for one of her employees, also a murder victim. Me and Paddy and the two guys who came with the hearse.

The cab companies were tired of me and Jordan didn't turn out to be Paddy's mystery visitor, so I declared the afternoon wasted and drove home, intending to waste the evening. That is, I went there to begin the assignment given to me by Decker. My walk down memory lane.

My house was on a short dead-end street that served a stretch of beach just wide enough to support that road to nowhere and about a dozen homes. At least, the number had been a dozen when the homes had all been modest summer rentals. Few of those original homes remained and, in a couple of cases, the missing ones had been torn down in pairs to make room for a single middle-class imitation of the mansions in Decker's neighborhood. Mine was original, if not totally original. Ella had had it remodeled in '61, and I now preserved it like a museum to that lost time, in spite of my neighbors' increasingly pointed recommendations on updates and additions and fresh paint.

I pulled the Continental into the carport that had until lately been decorated by Billy's surfboard, one of my museum's particular treasures. Unfortunately, I hadn't thought to chain that treasure to the wall, and it had been stolen. When Gabrielle had asked after it, I'd told her that I'd given the board to a kid who needed one, which was more or less true.

Decker had recommended a pitcher of Gibsons as a memory stimulant, but I didn't drink that much anymore and I'd never liked to mass-produce my cocktails. I preferred to use a shaker, though I usually stirred the gin and vermouth and ice. So, after I'd changed into my beachcomber disguise and started a small pile of briquettes flaming in the grill, I mixed a couple of Gibsons in a favorite shaker, an old metal one, dented and scarred. The Scott Elliott autograph model, Gabrielle called it. I selected a slightly newer glass, one of Swedish design that Ella had found. It flared at the top like a proper martini glass but had no stem or delicate base. In their place was a heavy glass plug that would keep a drink upright in anything short of a full gale. I shook a few cocktail onions into the glass, carried it and my shaker out onto the beach, and selected a likely spot. The sand was still quite warm, but when I dug down on the shaded side of my little dune, I soon hit a cool, damp layer. After filling my glass, I placed the shaker in the hole I'd dug and settled in.

There was an obvious alternative to delegating the Decker job and that was turning it down flat. I never considered the option seriously. For one thing, I wanted to know who was telling stories about the old con, and Amos Decker knew the answer. He was sworn to secrecy, but any man who mixed cocaine and laughing gas could be counted on to make a slip now and then. One slip would be all I'd need. And I had another reason for going ahead, a less rational one, suggested to me by an offbeat poet, my daughter. Gabby had observed that Paddy's murder made no sense in the present and therefore must have occurred in the past. I took her riddle to mean that, since there was no obvious motive in the present, the motive must be hidden in the past. And here, within a few weeks of Paddy's death, was a bit of that past come to tug on my sleeve in the form of Amos Decker.

That could have been a coincidence—had to be a coincidence in fact. All the dangerous types connected with the con were dead, at least the principal ones, the ones with skin in that ancient game. So there was no way that twenty-two-year-old sleight-of-hand could have gotten anyone killed in 1974. But if Paddy had taught me anything besides withholding evidence from the police and lock picking, it was that coincidences should always be given the gimlet eye.

It was early fall, which in Los Angeles meant that the heat had broken but the rains had yet to begin. Hollywood Security's offices were on Roe Street, in a low, tile-roofed building that looked like a movie-set hacienda and might even have been one once. As I had a young child and a beautiful wife who was anxious to have another, I was often late for the office's nine o'clock start time. On this particular morning, I was early and able to walk through the front door with my head held high, like a regular churchgoer on Easter morning.

That posture was risky, as it left my neck extended and vulnerable. I had that thought as soon as I saw the fire in Peggy Maguire's eyes. Peggy was Paddy's wife and office manager and governor, by which I mean the device that keeps an engine from running wild, the engine in question being Patrick J. Maguire's enthusiasm. Peggy was Paddy's opposite physically, short, thin, and dark, a fact that had served them well when they'd been a vaudeville team in the dim past. That she was also his opposite temperamentally served them equally well in business, Peggy being as adept at collecting an unpaid bill as Paddy was at picking up a check. At that moment, Peggy looked like she was more interested in collecting a scalp. Not mine, I was relieved to see when she finally noticed my entrance and relaxed the littlest bit.

"Scotty," she said, "thank God. You'll never believe who his nibs has in there. Someone he swore would never set foot in this office."

"Not Joe Stalin," I said, exposing my neck all over again.

"Guy De Felice," Peggy replied, hissing the end of the name, as the people who knew De Felice well routinely did.

He was a dweller in the Hollywood understory, if not the root system, a European of vague nationality who'd crossed the ocean to Mexico with the first refugee wave in the early days of the war and then somehow got across the border into California. One of the downsides of the movie business is that it attracts artists and con artists in roughly equal numbers, so naturally De Felice, one of the latter, had made his way to Hollywood to prey on the former. At first he'd done his preying as a kind of talent scout, his clients being honest refugees, dizzy enough from their relocation to accept De Felice as a valuable contact. That was strike one against the little man, as far as Paddy was concerned. When the war ended and the refugee dodge dried up, De Felice hung out his shingle as a "private inquiry agent," which was strike number two, since Paddy considered everything south of San Francisco to be his territory. Strike three was the specialty De Felice adopted: divorce cases, the messier the better. Paddy wouldn't touch a divorce.

All in all, I would have been less surprised if Peggy had confirmed that Stalin himself sat beyond Paddy's double doors. I muttered something consoling and started to edge toward the operatives' bullpen, where I hung my hat whenever it and I weren't out on the street. Peggy circled her desk and headed me off, taking my hat and turning me toward Paddy's office.

"Get in there and even the odds," she said.

I would have asked what she meant but she was already throwing open the doors, providing all the explanation I needed. Paddy and De Felice weren't the only two occupants of the sanctum sanctorum. Sitting beside De Felice on the visitor side of Paddy's big desk was a woman. That was all I could tell at first glance, except that she was raven-haired and had well-tanned shoulders.

Then Paddy said, "Scotty, just the man we need."

The woman turned in her chair and smiled at me, the smile, magnified by a wide swath of red lipstick, suggesting that I was just the man indeed. I checked my left ring finger with my left thumb to verify that I'd remembered to wear my wedding band.

"Mrs. Mariutto, allow me to introduce my top operative, Scott Elliott. Scotty, Rosa Mariutto. You already know Guy, of course."

Hearing Paddy refer to De Felice by his first name was such a shock I was slow to take Mariutto's proffered hand. I made up for that by holding it too long, which amused her, if I was still reading her lips correctly. She was wearing her black hair up and tucked beneath a broad-brimmed hat that shaded her gray eyes. The shade might have accounted for the steely quality of those eyes. And then again, maybe not.

De Felice had stood and was holding out his hand like a spaniel who expected a treat. I shook it, grimly.

De Felice had a spaniel's melancholy eyes and an adolescent's moustache, one that was all ends and no middle. But his memorable feature was his smile, his teeth being browner than last year's leaves. He wore a lot of brilliantine in his hair and cheap cologne everywhere else. It was currently wrestling with Rosa's expensive perfume and winning on points.

Paddy pointed me to a chair in the neutral ground at one end of his desk. "Have a seat. Mrs. Mariutto was just telling me about her problem, which is a unique one, in my experience."

That was saying something, so Mrs. Mariutto's capsule description of her unique problem was a major letdown: "I want to divorce my husband, and I can't."

That flummoxed me for a couple of reasons: first, that Paddy was considering a divorce case and, second, that Rosa Mariutto needed any help getting one. Divorce was a way of life in Hollywood. Ella had once joked that our local marriage licenses came with divorce applications printed on their obverse sides.

"No grounds?" I asked, fishing.

"Plenty of those," De Felice said with a little giggle. "My trusty Leica and I provided enough motel photos for a dozen divorces. I have them here if you'd care to—"

"Save them for your next stag party," Paddy suggested. To me, he said. "It might help if I tell you that Mrs. Mariutto's—"

"Rosa, please."

"That Rosa's husband is Ted Mariutto."

"Nope," I said.

"Oh, I forgot. You were out of town for the most interesting part of the forties. Well, while you were touring Europe at Uncle Sam's expense, Ted Mariutto—Moose Mariutto in those days—was having a high old time here in Los Angeles. He was taking advantage of a little program the government set up to support the war effort. It was called rationing."

"That I've heard of," I said.

"Since certain items were in short supply and high demand, black markets naturally sprang up. The man to see around here if you needed a nice steak or a tank of gas and found yourself low on points or coupons was Moose. He could get you anything for a price, but his specialty was gasoline. He dealt in stolen coupons, some lifted from the government's stockpile. Later he printed his own, and they would have fooled FDR himself."

"Okay," I said, "so he was a black marketeer. If you'll excuse the expression," I added to his wife.

"I've called him a lot worse," she assured me. "And this black-market business was before my time anyway. Ted and I didn't marry until 1949. In Omaha."

Paddy explained. "When the war ended, Moose's doctor recommended a change of climate."

"Dr. Morrie Bender," De Felice said and giggled again.

That name I knew. Nothing happened in the LA syndicate without Morrie Bender's say so. "I take it the cure worked."

"Yes," Paddy said. "A case of time healing a heel. Not only is Ted Mariutto back in town, he's set himself up as a producer at Warner Bros. No points for guessing whose influence got him that soft spot. Which brings us back to Rosa's divorce."

I tried another cast. "You can't get a divorce because Morrie Bender said no."

"No," Rosa said. "Morrie doesn't get involved in stuff like that. No, I can't get one because Ted's holding something over my head. It's a hobby of his, getting something on the people around him that he can use to control them. I never dreamt he'd pull that on me. Not until I showed him the pictures Guy took and told him I wanted out."

"Did Moose have a few photos of his own?" Paddy asked, his deferential tone softening the question not one bit.

Luckily, Rosa laughed it off. "Of me in action, you mean? No.

His leverage concerns my father, George Yowell. Daddy's in the beef business. During the war, he was one of Ted's sources for under-the-counter beef, though I didn't know that at the time. Daddy made a lot of money at that, and Ted has a record of every nickel. He's told me if I go ahead with the divorce, he'll send everything to the newspapers back in Omaha. That'll kill Daddy."

"It won't do your husband's reputation any good either," I said. "He's bluffing."

De Felice started clicking his tongue before I'd finished speaking. "Scotty, Scotty, Scotty. I admire your ability to work so long in this town and remain so . . . unsullied. Do you imagine Ted Mariutto's name will appear on any of these documents? He's far too clever for that."

"Too shifty," Rosa said. "I thought Guy here could get the records for me, but . . ."

"I was asked to do the extraordinary," De Felice said, "and I did it extraordinarily well."

I waited for Paddy to respond to that, perhaps by throwing something. But the great man was busy winding his watch, which gave De Felice a chance to brag some more.

"I entered the Mariutto apartment, with Rosa's able assistance, and Ted Mariutto's business office, with no one's assistance but my own."

Paddy interrupted. "His office on the Warners lot?"

"No. He maintains his own establishment near Wilshire and San Vicente. I searched both his home and office from the floorboards up and even opened his home and office safes. There wasn't a scrap of paper bearing the name of Rosa's beloved father."

"Any blackmail material on anyone else?" Paddy asked casually. "No."

At the risk of being called unsullied again, I repeated my first guess. "He's bluffing, like I said."

"There's another possibility," Paddy said. "I heard a story about Moose a week or two back. According to my source, he was in Cyrano's having a drink with pals from his racketeering days. A few drinks in fact. He was heard to brag that he'd stashed away a supply of counterfeit gas coupons against the day rationing comes back."

Rosa was nodding so hard her broad hat was stirring up a breeze. "I've heard him say that too, more than once."

"Any sign of those in one of his safes, Guy?"

"No," De Felice said. "No room for them. Both safes are compact."

"That settles it," Paddy said. "Moose Mariutto has another stash somewhere. All we have to do is find it."

"How?" I asked. "There are thousands of safe deposit boxes between here and Omaha."

"Moose wouldn't use a bank box. They're also small, and the cops can get into one with a court order. No, he has his own private hidey hole somewhere, take my word on it. As to how we'll find it, Moose will show us right where it is, with the right persuasion."

Ever since Paddy's bout of stem winding, Rosa had been checking her own watch. Not subtly either; its collar of stones flashed in the morning light every time she raised her wrist.

"Look, boys," she said, "I have to leave. I don't want Ted to figure out I'm not at my manicurist."

"Fine," Paddy said. "We three will put our heads together and let you know what we work out."

De Felice announced that he was walking his client to her car. That left Paddy and me alone for a few quiet words. Paddy got in the first ones, as usual.

"Like this tie? The guy who sold it to me swore it was cut from Dorothy Lamour's Sunday sarong."

"I haven't liked anything since I walked in here," I said. "Why are we working a divorce case? And with Guy De Felice? You once said you wouldn't use a sidewalk after he'd been on it."

"True," Paddy said. "His name ends with lice, and anyone who deals with him long enough ends the same way."

"So?"

Paddy leaned back in his chair with his hands behind his head. "Let's just say I'm a sucker for a damsel in distress."

CHAPTER EIGHT

I didn't report to Decker's the next day until after lunch, and even that was too early. The kid mogul was at home and was even up and about, but he was still shaking off the previous evening. From the looks of him, it must have been a wild one. His eyes—sans sunglasses today—had a yellow tinge, and his skin—what I could see of it above the collar of his terrycloth robe—resembled parchment. His curly mane was flat on one side, like someone had cut off a slice of it. Even his beard looked fried and fragile. All in all, he was the oldest twenty-something I'd ever seen, outside of a mummy case.

We talked far away from the sun, in the conversation pit in the living room. The room was still a mess, but the glass table at its center was now as clean as any operating theater. Polly Hayden might have done it; she'd been mortified by the cocaine dust the day before. I couldn't ask her because she wasn't there. Bimbo, the houseguest from hell, was. That is, I could hear someone his size stalking around off stage. But he never appeared.

I likewise couldn't ask Hayden whether the previous night's revels had been another celebration of Decker's preview or a reaction to a tough day with the studio brass. I asked Decker instead, indirectly.

"Rugged night?"

"Party at Frank Coppolini's."

Coppolini was another of the New Wave group, one who was

turning out hit after hit. Decker alluded to that success next, also indirectly.

"Frank's thinking of investing in Windjammer, my production company. He's interested in *The Shuffle*. He's done pretty well with gangster movies, as I'm sure you know."

Decker's voice sounded as friable as his beard looked. I decided he'd damaged it yelling his pitch over the roar of Coppolini's stereo.

"The studio brass weren't handing out blank checks yesterday?"

Decker winced slightly at that reprise of his recent boasting.

"No," he said, "the assholes. Look, Elliott, I need to know if you're serious about this. Are you ready to come across with some information?"

"Yes."

"We'll see. Let's play a little Twenty Questions. I'll ask and you answer. Name of the mark?"

"You know that already."

"I'm asking, you're answering."

"Ted Mariutto, a.k.a. Moose Mariutto. Black marketeer and sometime blackmailer."

"Who came up with the con?"

"Patrick J. Maguire, president of Hollywood Security."

"And his client was?"

"Mariutto's ex-wife, Rosa. She's still alive and kicking, by the way. She may not like being the subject of a movie."

I watched Decker for a reaction. All I got was a shrug that barely stirred his terrycloth cocoon.

"Don't worry. The names will be changed to protect the innocent filmmaker."

Suddenly Decker's yellowed eyes were watching my clear blue ones very closely. "What was the objective of the con?"

Every question he'd asked had seemed like a test, this one especially. "Some papers Mariutto was using to keep his wife on the reservation."

Something about my answer amused him. I thought he might tell me why. I kept talking to encourage him, and that was a mistake, as my chatter sent him off on a tangent.

"The papers had to do with the black market in beef during the war."

"The war," Decker repeated with a little sneer. "You old guys kill me. You don't think you even have to name your war, it was such a big fucking deal. Like we never had a war before it. Like we haven't had two since, not counting the cold one. The center of the universe, that's your generation."

"Don't get jealous on me. You're green enough in the gills right now."

Decker winced again. "You don't know the half of it. Who was Hollywood Security partnered with?"

"Guy De Felice, a sleazy private detective."

"There's another kind?"

That line sounded familiar, but I couldn't place it. I got out my tobacco pouch and pipe and started to move cavendish from one to the other. It was just some innocent stage business, designed to give me time to work up my comeback. Decker reacted like I'd pulled a knife.

"Don't, Elliott, you'll kill me. I'm close to puking up a kidney right now. I'm sorry about the crack. Other private eyes are crooked, but you're straighter than John Wayne's rifle barrel."

"Let's not go overboard." I put the pouch and pipe away.

"Thanks. Last question for today. Did the con work?"

"Last question? I just got here."

"I'll pay for the whole day, don't worry. Right now I have to take some medicine and lie down."

I decided to strike a blow for the absent Polly Hayden, who evidently saw something in Decker that I'd so far missed. "You're going at this hard living too hard. You prove you're a genius by your work, not by how fast you kill yourself."

"And you know about geniuses how?"

"Mostly from bailing them out of bad decisions."

"Listen, Elliott, people who live nice, simple lives turn out nice, simple, made-for-TV movies. If you want your work to be remembered, to have an edge, that's where you have to live, on the edge. That's the pact my generation has made with fame. Some of us will die young, sure, but the ones who don't will be accepting Oscars for lifetime achievement in twenty years. One of those survivors will be me.

"Now, back to my question. Did the con work?"

I'd had the impression all along that Decker was checking my information against some mental list, comparing my answers to ones he already had, maybe to double-check his original source, more likely to double-check me. So I stuck to the truth.

"Yes," I said. "The con worked."

Decker settled downward in his seat like the air was coming out of him. "We're going to have some interesting talks you and I. See you tomorrow."

Amos Decker had given me the rest of the day off, but I didn't take it. I took a drive instead, to beautiful Thousand Oaks, a little way northwest of Los Angeles. Thousand Oaks was a rare thing, a planned community that had actually stuck to its plan. The result was a very beautiful, very expensive place to live, the beauty coming from the many trees that gave the city its name and from the Conejo Valley itself, a little piece of the Mediterranean coast that had been set down in Ventura County by mistake.

I was there to see Rosa Mariutto, now Rosa Wardell. Her second husband, Jack Wardell, had been one of the developers of the area, which is how I'd kept track of Rosa over the years. I was used to seeing her by his side in newspaper photos publicizing the opening of a new subdivision or shopping center. The most recent photo had shown Rosa as a widow, dedicating Jack Wardell Park.

Earlier I said that there were two living women who could have told Decker about the Mariutto con and that one was Ella. The other was Rosa Wardell. That's why I'd paid careful attention to Decker when I'd mentioned her. As far as I could tell, he hadn't reacted at all.

I didn't sneak up on Mrs. Wardell the way I had on Ella, in part because I was more confident that Rosa would see me. I called ahead, and the widow gave me directions to her home off Thousand Oaks Boulevard.

It wasn't as grand a house as I'd expected, but it was very nice, a ranch with as many gables as a Tudor and exposed exterior beams like a Tudor as well. When I turned into the brick drive, I saw Rosa in the front yard, collecting an armful of the flowers she'd been named after. She was on the happier side of fifty, by my rough calculation, but looked about ten years younger, in spite of a tan that would have made a tennis pro jealous. She was dressed in tennis whites at the moment, in fact, the ensemble a knit top, a short, pleated skirt, and a white kerchief tied across her hair. The hair was no longer black, and its new color was hard to pin down, as it was heavily frosted. We had that in common, though my frosting had been applied by Mother Nature.

Our other link was that conference in Paddy's office in 1952. More specifically, that we were the only survivors of that conference. Peggy, the eavesdropper beyond the double doors, had died peacefully from the complications of a stroke in 1969. De Felice had died violently in 1962, after one of his sleaziest deals had blown up. Rosa mentioned our other murdered alumnus as soon as I climbed out of the Continental.

"I'm so sorry about poor Mr. Maguire. I thought he'd live forever."

"So did he."

I extended my condolences regarding her husband as she led me inside to a comfortable study that overlooked the backyard pool. It was decorated with Jack Wardell's tennis and golf trophies. Or so I thought until Rosa went off to make us tea. To pass the wait, I gave the hardware a closer look and saw that most of the plaques and cups belonged to my hostess.

She returned carrying two tall, frosted glasses. Being a trained observer, I noted that the front of her white polo shirt, which had previously been secured by two of its three buttons, was now making do with one.

"Too early in the day for tea," she said. "I try never to drink it before sundown."

Rosa's mid afternoon alternative was a Tom Collins.

I took in more with my first sip than I'd intended when she said, "I thought you might be calling me for a date. I was hoping I'd made a lasting impression in '52. But I see you're still married."

I could have hedged on that, but not without creating an impression of my own, a false one. "I'm here about the job we did for you back then. It's bobbed to the surface again."

I told her all about the very well-informed Amos Decker and his embryo movie.

Rosa said, "You thought I might be the bean spiller? Scotty, the whole charade was set up to protect my father. Daddy's ninety-two and ornery as ever. I'd be the last person selling that secret, even if I needed the money, which I don't. What about that crazy little keyhole peeper I got hooked up with, Guy De Felice? He'd sell his mother's secrets."

"Dead."

Rosa thought about it while she chewed on a maraschino cherry. "There's nobody else then. I mean, some of Ted's old gang may still be around. Al Alsip, maybe. But that doesn't help us. No one on Ted's side of the net even knew there was a con. And I sure haven't told anybody. I've never wanted anyone around here to know I was ever married to Ted, never mind what I had to do to get unmarried."

"Who recommended Hollywood Security to you in the first place?"

It might have been De Felice—had almost certainly been De Felice—but it wouldn't hurt to check. If some long-lost friend from Rosa's days as Mrs. Mariutto had sent her our way in 1952, Rosa might have rewarded her with a full report and then forgotten about it.

The widow was smiling at me. It wasn't exactly Decker's smug smile, but it was too close to it for comfort.

"You really don't know, do you? Mr. Maguire was a sly old dog."

"What don't I know?"

"That I didn't contact Hollywood Security. Hollywood Security contacted me. Paddy did, out of the blue. He said he'd heard about my trouble and offered to help. He had an old score to settle with Ted; he didn't say over what. Knowing Ted, I had no trouble believing there was one.

"Paddy had a couple of conditions. I couldn't tell anyone that he'd approached me, especially not Guy. I was supposed to call up and make an appointment like any old client. But I was for certain to bring Guy with me.

"I was sure you were in on it, Scotty. Sorry."

Not half as sorry as I was. I took another sip of my drink and then planted my glass on its coaster. "Thanks for your time," I said.

Rosa was fingering the last functioning button on her blouse. "No need to run off."

Just then, running off seemed like the better part of valor. But I held my ground long enough to ask one more question.

"When did you last see Paddy?"

"The last time in person? 1952."

CHAPTER NINE

I left Thousand Oaks less sure of things than I'd been on my drive in. Like Rosa Wardell, I had no trouble believing that Paddy and Mariutto had crossed paths sometime during the war and that Paddy had felt afterwards that there was a debt to collect. But that still left the problem of Guy De Felice. Back in 1952, I'd barely been able to credit that Paddy had accepted the little operator as a part of the Rosa Mariutto package deal, even though I'd seen him do it with my own eyes. But now Rosa was asking me to believe something even less likely, that when it would have been easy to cut De Felice out, Paddy had intentionally dealt him in.

And yet. One of the things I'd never liked about working for Paddy was that he could be as tight with information as Ebenezer Scrooge was with anthracite. It had been Paddy's method of retaining control of a case or maybe just his nature. His tendency to hold things back had often given me the feeling I was working with one eye closed. Sometimes both eyes. I could remember more than one angry march into his office after I'd been embarrassed or even endangered by not knowing the whole setup. Those memories were so clear and the current heat under my collar so familiar that, from old habit, I headed to Roe Street now.

When the kids had been little, a favorite pastime of mine had been driving them around Los Angeles, pointing out the famous old places that were still there and even the ones that weren't, the ones that had given way to bank branches and parking lots. Billy had called the latter stops "Dad's guided tour of things that aren't there anymore."

The old Hollywood Security hacienda now qualified for that tour. In its old spot on Roe Street, there stood a modest and nondescript office building, the home of an insurance company that had recently—by an odd twist of fate—been a client of the new Hollywood Security's. Seeing our old address on the insurance company's letterhead had given me a mild shock. Seeing its headquarters now in person was a replay of that, the time I'd spent on Roe Street in memory the evening before having weakened my grip on the present.

I parked in my old spot at the curb and crossed the insurance company's concrete forecourt to the court's centerpiece, a burbling fountain. It was as angular and unmemorable as the building behind it, but its rectangular perimeter had a broad stone edge the width of a park bench. That stone bench was a popular break spot, to judge from the number of cigarettes ground out on the pavement around it. Just then, though, I had it to myself. I took out the pipe I'd frightened Decker with, tapped out the now dry tobacco, and refilled it.

I couldn't barge into Paddy's office and demand an explanation of his approach to Rosa Mariutto. So I did the next best thing, which was also the natural thing, given where I was sitting. I returned to that conference in 1952, looking for clues.

When De Felice came back from seeing Rosa to her car, Paddy lit the smoking lamp by taking out a fresh corona. I dug out my pack of Lucky Strikes, hoping to ward off a little of De Felice's cologne. The private inquiry agent didn't produce any tobacco of his own, but at the sight of ours he searched his pockets until he found a box of licorice tabs, the nicotine-laced kind that were marketed to smokers trying to quit. Those explained the mystery of the brown teeth.

The mystery of De Felice's continuing presence was another matter. Paddy could have dismissed him the minute Rosa announced her departure. Instead, he'd included him in our follow-up bull session. He even let De Felice take the floor, by pretending to be preoccupied with the lighting of his cigar.

"Gentlemen," De Felice began, "the challenge before us is to discover the location of Mariutto's hiding place—or hidey hole, as Mr. Maguire put it so, ah, whimsically. So what do we do? What I propose is this: We use Mariutto's known habits against him. We know from the lovely Rosa's story that her husband likes to collect compromising information about those closest to him. We also know, because I failed to find any trace of such material, that Mariutto must keep it in his hidey hole. I suggest we offer to sell him some dirt on a current associate, something he won't be able to resist. Then we wait for him to lead us to his cache."

It wasn't a bad idea, I hated to admit. "Something on Morrie Bender, say," I kicked in.

Paddy and De Felice said no as a chorus. The little divorce specialist actually paled.

"By no means, Scotty. It's too dangerous. That would be using an atom bomb to smother a fire. No. I was thinking of an associate from Mariutto's new life as a movie producer. He's producing through Warner Bros. Our best course would be to offer him something on the man he would most like to control, his new boss, Jack Warner.

"I am confident that you can acquire such information, Mr. Maguire, given your vast network of contacts. You might even have it at your fingertips. I seem to recall hearing that you two were heavily involved when a Warner Bros. screenwriter was accused of being a communist a few years ago. If Jack Warner tried to protect that unfortunate soul, it would be quite compromising in the current political climate. Mariutto could not resist such a morsel."

De Felice was all but licking his chops himself. I thought he could be a serious rival to Mariutto in the blackmail business, given the chance.

Paddy Maguire, who was not above filing away the odd tidbit himself, sat considering De Felice's idea for as long as it took him to blow three perfect smoke rings.

Then he said, "No. It's not a bad idea. It's a good one, in fact, but the timing's too loose. Moose would have no particular reason to add this morsel to his secret cache on our schedule. We have to assume the cache is somewhere out-of-the-way if no one stumbled on it the whole time he was in Omaha. And out-of-the-way means inconvenient. Moose might keep whatever we sold him in his home or office safe for weeks or even months just to save himself that inconvenience. In fact, he'd probably keep it close to hand on purpose, if he anticipated some interference from Jack Warner. He'd be a fool not to anticipate that, given the gentleman's reputation.

"No, we can't afford to keep tabs on him forever. We'll have to think again. Scotty, you're up. We need a standup double at least."

For once, I was sure I could reach third. "We use something else we know is in that cache: the gas rationing coupons. The fighting in Korea is dragging on with no end in sight. We convince Mariutto that gas rationing is coming back. All it would take is a story planted in the local paper by some editor who owes us a favor. We say that, to save time, the government is planning to use its own stored supply of ration coupons from the forties. That would make Mariutto's counterfeits gold again. He'd bring them out of the icebox—or at the very least check on them—and we'd have him."

Paddy was looking at me as proudly as he had the first time I'd jimmied a Yale lock. But he didn't even grant me three smoke rings worth of consideration.

"Your plan has a certain epic sweep, Scotty. C.B. De Mille himself would grant you that. You're willing to scare the city and state and even the country, once the wire services picked up the story, just to prod one ex-racketeer. Not to mention getting a tame journalist fired, if we could find one tame enough to go along."

"We plant newspaper stories all the time without getting anyone fired."

"Yes, we float the kind of balloons every Hollywood publicist floats. We say an actor who has a secret boyfriend and is nervous about it is actually dating Jane Russell. Or that an actress who just made the papers for biting her maid is planning to adopt quintuplets. Nobody in this town takes that kind of light fiction seriously. But an unattributed claim about gas rationing would surely get somebody—several somebodies—the boot. And those somebodies would be pointing to us pretty damn quick. Worse, the story would be officially denied so fast Mariutto would never have a chance to act.

"Still, I like the idea of using the counterfeit coupons. Being a patriot, I hate to think Mariutto got away with hawking those—statute of limitations be damned. But I suggest we use them for what they are: incriminating evidence, evidence Moose was a fool to hang on to.

"Guy, when you were touring Mariutto's home and office, did you come across any tax returns?"

"Yes. He keeps them in his office on Wilshire. I made photographic copies of the latest ones for Rosa."

"Good." Paddy pulled a notebook from his desk and, after consulting it, dialed a number on the phone connected to his private line. I seldom saw Paddy actually dial a phone and I wondered why he hadn't placed this call through Peggy.

Then he said, "Is this the Los Angeles office of the IRS? I'd like to report a tax evader here in town. No, I don't care to give my name. The cheat's name is Ted Mariutto. Of Ted Mariutto Productions. During the war, he made a pile of money selling black-market gasoline, money never reported to you. He's still living off that unreported cash. It isn't right." Paddy then spelled Mariutto's name and cradled the handset.

"That should produce solid results. They'll refer the matter to Washington or handle it themselves. Either way, Moose should be hearing from them. Guy, I'll need you and your Leica to revisit his place of business. I want copies of as many of his tax returns as you can lay your hands on, preferably from the war years."

"A return visit will be extremely risky," De Felice murmured.

"For which risk you'll be abundantly compensated. In addition to whatever Rosa is paying you, you'll get thirty-three cents of every dollar we take from Mariutto."

I almost dropped my Lucky. "We're going after Mariutto's money, too?"

"Of course. We've got to recoup our expenses somehow. 'The laborer is worthy of his hire,' as the good book says."

Paddy assumed a look of shocked amazement. It was every bit as lifelike as Charlie McCarthy's left leg. "I hope you weren't thinking we'd take money from a damsel in distress, Scotty. That would be ungallant.

"But remember this, gentlemen. The only safe con is one the mark never tumbles to. That's especially true when the mark is as well connected as Moose Mariutto. Our goal is Rosa free and Moose none the wiser. Now, to your posts."

CHAPTER TEN

Amos Decker hadn't mentioned a specific time for our next talk. Any reasonable person would have assumed he'd meant the same time he'd set for our prior meeting, the vague "after lunch." A more generous person, remembering how wasted he'd still been at that meeting, would have granted him another hour or two in intensive care.

I wasn't feeling reasonable or generous. When I got up the day after my drive to Thousand Oaks, I was feeling the way some of the locals do when the Santa Ana winds start to roar down the canyons: itchy and wary and wrathful.

Hoping to shake the mood, I went out for breakfast, to a little diner near a fishing pier. An acquaintance of mine had used the pier to drive himself into the ocean, way back when I'd been an actor and Paddy had been a studio guard. Paddy and I had gone down together to look into it and later eaten at the diner, which Paddy had called "a dog wagon." The place had changed hands several times since then and maybe even the grease in its fryer. Ella would never set foot in it, but there were always people there and loud talking and that's what I wanted.

I sat eating eggs and bacon and looking at a sports page I wasn't really reading. Behind me, three college-age guys were arguing over whether President Nixon would be impeached. One of the debaters used the phrase "begging the question" incorrectly. That is, he used it to mean "raising the question," when it actually identified an error in logic, an argument whose premise took its conclusion for granted. "Begging the question" was misused more often than not anymore, understandably, since it accurately described what the people who got it wrong were trying to say and had never really conveyed the meaning logic teachers had given it. The first guy who'd gotten it wrong in my hearing, at least on a regular basis, had been Paddy. Nor had he been open to correction, which I'd once foolishly attempted.

"I congratulate you on your thorough grounding in logic," he'd replied on that occasion. "I look forward to seeing some signs of it in your work."

I had the same hope for my current work, my real work, finding Paddy's killer. I was wasting time in memory, some of those memories gin-soaked, instead of working out exactly why Paddy had been in that alley. The problem was he hadn't left me anything to work with, not even a vague and unlikely storybook clue, like a half-burned page in an incinerator or a word written in blood. And, if I was right, he'd left me in the dark deliberately.

After breakfast, I drove to Decker's beach house, expecting to find him hungover again. Hoping for it, actually. The price of my leaving him in peace today would be the name of his secret source. I'd get it if I had to play bongo drums until he gave in.

The first sign that even that modest goal was beyond reach was the empty space where Decker's Eldorado had been parked on my prior visits. That suggested that Decker was sleeping off his last snort or swallow somewhere else. I might not have stopped at all if it hadn't been for the presence of another car, a silver Mercedes-Benz 450slc in the spot next to Decker's empty one. The coupe had been there on my first visit and so could have belonged to Polly Hayden. On the strength of that guess, I parked and climbed out.

I was thinking about how I might talk Hayden into giving me a few minutes alone in Decker's office when I heard her scream. I was certain it was Hayden and not because of my deduction about the Mercedes. In the last picture of hers I'd seen, she'd screamed the very same way when her outlaw lover had been machine-gunned by the police.

As I ran to the front steps, I caught sight of a neighbor standing open-mouthed on her patio. She was dressed in a bikini and squeezing a small dog to her chest.

"Call the police," I yelled to her.

The front door was solid and sporting three locks. I hit it hard just to prove to myself that it wouldn't give, and it sprang open with the sound of splintering wood.

I slid to a halt in the living room as Hayden screamed again. She was on the floor near the sliding doors to the deck, on her back, with Bimbo astride her and bent forward, his face just above hers. He was tearing at her blouse with one hand and stifling a third scream with the other.

That left him with no hand to block the kick I aimed as his shaggy head. I landed enough of it to knock my shoe off, but the blow barely laid Bimbo over on his side. He sat up before I could pin him down, and I saw why he hadn't reacted to the crash of the door. He was high on something, his eyes bloodshot and vacant. Until he focused them on me. Then their red color was the perfect shade for his rage.

He sprang for me, but he and Hayden tangled legs and he nearly went down again. I hit him hard, square in the face, and broke his nose. I followed up with a right that should have ended the dance, drugs or no drugs, but Bimbo grabbed my fist and then my shoulder and launched me across the room. I landed face down, half in the conversation pit and half out. Bimbo settled the question by kicking me down its single step. I upended the mirrored table getting to my feet and then pushed it over into Bimbo's path.

I scrambled out of the pit to the sound of glass shattering. Hayden had disappeared as completely as she had at Avenal five years before. I had just enough time to notice that before Bimbo came up at me, his fists held low, his face running with blood. I had a second's flashback to a fight in an Indiana forest against another big man, one with no face to speak of. Then Bimbo was launching a roundhouse right at my head. I stepped inside it and landed a combination that finally got his attention and then another, after he'd creased the side of my head with a second sidearm blow. All the time I was backing toward the only daylight I could see, which streamed in from the balcony with the million-dollar view.

At that point, Bimbo decided to give up boxing and go back to wrestling. He opened his hands and lunged at me, going down on his hands and knees when I dodged aside. I kept going, out through the open door to the balcony. I was out of shape and feeling it. It'd been years since I'd hit anyone and a lot longer than that since I'd met a man with as much bone in his head as Bimbo.

I was gauging a jump down to the sand when I spotted Hayden. She was crouched next to the sliding door, holding the wooden dowel rod that dead-bolted the slider at night. I grabbed it from her and started swinging it while I still had my back to the thud of Bimbo's approaching steps. The rod was as thick as the middle of a pool cue. I'd been on the receiving end of one of those, but the memory didn't make me hold back. I swung for the center field fence and broke my bat on a shaggy fast ball.

Even then, Bimbo didn't fall down, but he did stagger through the living room howling. At once, Hayden was trying to talk between sobs.

"Amos flew to Vegas. I thought he took everyone with him. I came over to get some things. Bimbo jumped me as soon as I came through the door."

I didn't try to quiet her until I could get her outside, where we'd both have been safer, because I could hear an approaching siren. I'd been hearing it for a while without having had time to note it. A car braked hard at the front steps, and the helpful neighbor shouted instructions over the barking of her dog.

Then Bimbo reentered the living room, his head bloody top and bottom, his eyes bloody in between. He was holding a forty-four magnum, a movie gun I'd grown to hate. I had time to step between it and Hayden before he fired. The big pistol bucked on him, and the bullet hit the glass sliding door above my head and to the right. He was adjusting his aim when a voice from the front doorway told him to drop it.

The cop's friendly warning gave Bimbo a chance to try his luck one more time. He dropped the cannon instead.

CHAPTER ELEVEN

Hayden gave her statement to the second responders like it was the script pages she'd memorized for that day's filming. The first responders had taken Bimbo to a hospital, one with barred windows I hoped. The police asked about the drugs Bimbo obviously was on. Hayden was vague about their source and the officers let her be, since she had a face and a name they knew. She was more specific about meaningless things like the front door, mentioning in passing that she'd only set the button lock on the knob when she'd entered and not its several deadbolts. That detail was meaningless because Bimbo had already been inside the house, but it did explain how an aging security operative had been able to crash through the door like George Reeves through a cardboard wall.

After the official questioners had left, it was my turn. I started with Amos Decker's trip to Las Vegas.

"That's just Amos," Hayden said. "He should be here, making sure the studio releases his cut of his movie, so naturally he's off partying. Later, when the movie tanks, he'll blame the studio editors who recut it. He'll call them hacks, but they're more disciplined than he is, just not as talented. Amos doesn't see that having a special talent doesn't get you life achievement awards. Showing up every day does."

She then segued smoothly to an unrelated subject. "Thanks for showing up today, Scotty. I'm sorry it got you beaten up."

"That's my special talent," I said. "Why aren't you in Vegas?"

"Because Amos is tired of my nagging. Because I've got my own awards to earn. Because Amos is throwing me over for a younger woman. Take your pick."

"The one about the younger woman true?"

Hayden shrugged. "He hasn't admitted it yet, but that's the way things work out here. The studio will throw me over for a younger woman too, if I don't show it I've got more than youth to sell.

"Amos doesn't see that threat either. None of these film school wonders do. They don't seem to remember that the film schools turn out a new class every year. If Amos and the others want to keep their spots, they have to do good work, now, while they have a chance."

"Speaking of Decker's work," I said, "what do you know about *The Shuffle?*"

"I know it's the latest shiny object that's caught Amos's eye. And I know he's counting on you to supply him with background. I really didn't know that when you came here that first day. Honest, Scotty."

"Do you know where he came across the idea?"

"No, honest."

She surprised me then by giving me the same maternal look she'd used when apologizing for my bruises. "Don't get your hopes up over this movie. Amos gets a lot of can't miss ideas. The latest one is always the best."

I would have told her that I hadn't gotten my hopes up over a movie since her mother last wore bobby socks, but she veered again, back to her own problems.

"I guess it's the same with lovers, the latest one is always the best."

"Not if you're going for a life achievement award," I said, though my own had been recalled by the Academy. "What now?"

"I finish what I came here to do, collect my stuff and clear out. Would you mind waiting around while I do it?"

I told her I'd stay. In exchange, I asked for directions to Decker's office. She led me to one of the ocean-view bedrooms.

"You would've had to fight Bimbo all over again to get in here, if the cops hadn't hauled him off. He guarded this room like a bulldog."

Bimbo might have been protective of Decker's drug paraphernalia. I found enough of it after Hayden left me to supply a small college dormitory. What I didn't find were any notes on *The Shuffle*. There were plenty of scripts lying around. I'd never met a producer or director who didn't have those to burn. None of Decker's concerned a con game, not in 1952 or any other year.

I found some correspondence connected with the production company he'd mentioned, Windjammer, and, in the same drawer, a book of checks bearing the company's name. I started backward in the checkbook's register but didn't have to go very far. Just a few days before Decker called Hollywood Security to request my services, he'd written a check for five thousand dollars to a Helen Gallimore.

I knew the name. I was sure of it, though I couldn't place it. I sat there listening to the surf boom and wishing I had Paddy or, better still, Peggy Maguire to ask. Paddy had rarely forgotten a name and Peggy never had. I decided to run through the names of the people connected with the con and that proved to be all the prod my memory needed. When I got to Ted Mariutto, I had Gallimore. She'd been his secretary. I'd only seen her once, but I was still surprised that I hadn't IDed her immediately. I was fairly certain that I'd forget landing on Utah Beach before I'd forget the day I met Helen Gallimore.

Hayden signaled me that she was ready by sounding the horn on her Mercedes. I found her standing next to it, the girl Friday she'd called to drive her home sitting behind the wheel. The amount of stuff they'd crammed into the car suggested that Hayden's relationship with Decker hadn't been a weekend fling. Even so, she was sniffle free as she stood looking up at the house. She was closer to tears when she hugged me good-bye and thanked me for standing by her.

"Thanks for standing by me," I said.

I drove home to change out of my suit and throw it away—it was that sprinkled with blood from Bimbo's busted nose. I had a visitor, one with a house key of her own, Gabrielle. She gave me another of her inherited looks when she saw the blood.

"I led with my left, I swear."

"I can tell by your swollen knuckles. Over Paddy?"

"No, over something else."

She didn't call me Mannix that morning, but the nickname would have fit for once. Before I'd left Decker's desk, I'd called Hollywood Security for a little of the legwork the television detective always turned over to his high-tech employer. Hodson McLean had encouraged me along those lines, after all. I'd asked Vickie to locate the current whereabouts of Helen Gallimore—there been no address or phone number for her in Decker's office—and any other information on her she could find.

I similarly delegated lunch. Gabrielle had it ready when I came out of the shower. She'd selected soft foods, in case my teeth were loose. While we ate, I explained the blood. The story didn't hold Gabby's interest, not even with Polly Hayden in a principal role. My daughter had brought along her own agenda, which she served as our dessert course.

"I heard you dropped in on Mom."

"That was business." I'd mentioned Amos Decker during my explanation of the fight but not how we'd met in the first place. I told Gabby now about Decker's wanting everything I could remember about a certain old case.

"Mom told me that and how you thought she might be the one who'd recommended Hollywood Security. I told her you'd just used it as an excuse to see her."

That was news to me, though it could still have been true. A character didn't always understand his own motivations. Ella the screenwriter had taught me that.

"And what did she say?"

We were seated across from one another in my breakfast nook, Gabby idly rubbing her thumb across the copper band on my wrist at the spot where her brother's name was engraved.

"I think she'd like you to stop by more often, but she might not realize it."

"So we're both acting unconsciously?"

"Everybody acts unconsciously, Dad." Gabby was another graduate of the Ella Elliott screenwriting school. "Take Paddy. He had a good reason to be in that alley that night, one he knew about. But he had other reasons he didn't know about."

That reminded me of Captain Grove's theory. "Maybe Paddy was after the big score that could have put him back on top."

"Maybe he was after what he found. Maybe he just hadn't admitted it to himself."

I sat there wishing that, if Paddy had gone into that alley hoping to die, it had been an unconscious hope.

Then Gabby said, "Why are you still wearing your wedding ring?"

"I'm self-conscious about my tan line."

"Dad."

"Your mother and I aren't divorced. Would you be happier if we were?"

"Less happy. But less confused."

"I guess I like to cling to a little happy even at the cost of a lot of confused."

Gabby nodded. "Mom's hurting again. She was getting better, but now she's not."

"I know," I said.

We did the dishes. I thought Gabby would say good-bye after that, citing some late school year or early summer break business. Instead, she said, "How much of this old story have you told Amos Decker?"

"Not much, yet. I'm still trying to remember it. And, as an audience, he's a moving target."

"Tell it to me," Gabby said.

"Why?"

"For practice. And because I'd like to hear it. It's set in 1952, you said? That should be an upbeat story. The old Hollywood Security was alive and kicking back then. Your later stories are too elegiac."

"I'll look that word up later."

"Do."

We sat out back, on my sandy concrete patio, and I recapped the conference in Paddy's office that had begun with Rosa Mariutto and Guy De Felice and ended with De Felice alone. When I'd finished the intro, I hesitated, and Gabby picked up on that.

"Reached terra incognito?"

"No. Just terra not cognitoed in a long time. Let's see. Where was I?"

CHAPTER TWELVE

Shortly after Paddy opened the con by phoning in his anonymous tip to the IRS, I spent a morning cleaning up a job Hollywood Security had undertaken for the English actor David Niven. I got back to our offices a little after one, but didn't make it inside. Not right away. On the front walk, I was collared by Detective Sergeant Walter Grove of the Los Angeles Police Department.

No man likes to have his lapel yanked, and I was especially sensitive about having mine yanked by Grove. For one thing, the cop made a habit of it. For another, he was a guy who oozed oil, his badly pitted face always shiny, his dark hair always matted. Grove laying hands on you was more than an insult. It was a dry cleaning challenge.

"Where've you been, Elliott? Out shaking down widows? Or was it orphans?"

"Always orphans on Tuesdays," I said. "Cigarette, Sergeant?"

I used the excuse of reaching for my Luckies to ease my coat from Grove's grasp. He wouldn't even look at the proffered pack.

"I hear Maguire has been sniffing around Ted Mariutto. Why?"

"Don't ask me," I said. "You know Paddy from way back. You know he keeps his own counsel."

The "way back" was a dig. Once upon a time, Grove had been on Paddy's payroll, in a manner of speaking. He'd accepted the odd bribe from Hollywood Security for providing inside information on police investigations. Once Grove had made that mistake, Paddy had owned him, since revealing their business relationship would have ended Grove's career. Then somehow, Grove had wiggled off Paddy's hook. How was a mystery I'd never been able to solve, but the business had left the policeman with an undying hatred for Hollywood Security and all who sailed in her.

"I know Maguire," Grove said. "I know you both, Elliott. I know your weakness for horning in on a murder case will be what finishes off your whole crooked outfit."

I paused in the act of lighting my cigarette. "What murder?" I was thinking of Rosa Mariutto, Paddy's damsel in distress, and holding my breath.

"You telling me you never heard of Sugar Stapert?"

I let my breath out in the form of a question. "Sugar who?"

"Sugar Stapert. She was a singer. She hung around Mariutto during the war, when he was nobody to hang around. In 1944, she was found shot to death in the roadhouse where she worked. Ring any bells?"

"Not bell one. Why would it? I was in Europe at the time, wearing a steel hat."

Grove gave me a look that felt like a frisk. "Maybe 'cause her murder got the kind of treatment Hollywood Security provides for a price. A cover-up."

"You think Paddy was involved in that?"

"If he was, he wasn't calling the shots. I think Mariutto's guardian angel, Morrie Bender, arranged it. But I don't know for sure. I only know the Stapert investigation was a joke. Mariutto was never even brought in for questioning."

"Why didn't you bring him in, Sergeant?"

"'Cause I was overseas myself at the time, knee-deep in sons of Nippon. And I liked them better than I do you."

I thought Grove might follow me inside to brace Paddy, but he turned on his heel and marched off. Not that I got to see my boss alone. Peggy nodded to the great man's office as I entered and held up two fingers. Then she nodded toward the double doors again, this time meaning that I was required within. I slipped inside under the cover of one of Paddy's booming laughs. The stealth was wasted, as Paddy announced me as soon as he sobered up.

"Scotty, there you are. Say hello to two old friends of yours."

I knew both of the men who turned in their seats, though I would never have presumed to call them friends. One was Max Froy, who'd been a house director at Warner Bros. since *The Jazz Singer* days. Like most house directors, Froy could do any kind of film, from gangster movies to swashbucklers. His only specialty was turning them out on time and under budget.

The other visitor was a movie star and therefore known to most of the country. He was Torrance Beaumont, an ex-crooner who played tough guys who were also heartthrobs, a parlay few actors could pull off. In real life, Beaumont was neither, being thin and balding and a collector of fine art. His other hobby was giving people a hard time, me especially.

I'd gotten to know Beaumont and Froy when Hollywood Security had worked the case Guy De Felice mentioned when we'd been pitching ideas for the con, the case of the Warners screenwriter accused of being a red. We'd done our damnedest to cover that up, until a murder had broken the whole thing wide open. Thinking of that cover-up and the murder reminded me of Grove's story about Sugar Stapert. I wanted Beaumont and Froy gone so I could ask Paddy about that, but the meeting wasn't close to wrapping up. Or so I calculated from the amount of Irish whiskey left in the three glasses on Paddy's desk.

"Join us?" he asked me, nodding at the bottle.

"No thanks," I said.

"Too early for you, Two Gun?" Beaumont asked, flashing his canines at me. "Or is it a redeye or nothing for you cowpokes?"

"Babysitting tonight," I said. I'd long since learned that the best way to handle Beaumont's ribbing was to roll with it. "Ella checks my breath and my guns at the door."

"Please give your lovely wife my regards," Froy said, his German accent making the remark sound more like a pleasantry and less like a proposition. What he said next made it clear that it had been a proposition, of sorts. "I hear through the local grapevine that she has written a new script that is a work of art. I would very much like the chance to speak to her about it."

I promised to pass on the message and settled in.

Beaumont said, "Now that we're all here, what's the big favor?"

Paddy had been in the act of lifting his glass. He set it down again.

"We're running a little operation on behalf of a young lady who's trapped in a bad marriage."

"There's another kind?" Beaumont asked. "Sorry, Two Gun. I forgot you're on the world's longest honeymoon."

"We need a certain party," Paddy continued, "to believe that Hollywood Security can fix a problem with the IRS."

"Can you?" Beaumont asked.

Paddy laughed again. "If I could, I'd be hiring myself out as a CPA. In this town, I could open a branch office on every block. No, this is strictly balloon juice, but we need to put it over."

"How?" Froy asked.

"By doing a little of what you gentlemen do for a living: storytelling. You have most of the lines, Max. I'd like you to go back to Warners Bros. and tell the likeliest gossips that Tory Beaumont had a big tax problem and that Hollywood Security made it go away. You don't know any of the details, except that it involved a good-sized pile of money changing hands.

"Tory, your job is easier. You're simply to confirm the broad outlines of the story, should anyone ask."

"Sounds simple enough," Beaumont said. "What's the catch?"

"The man most likely to ask is the catch. It should be Warners' newest producer, Ted Mariutto."

"Old Moose?" Beaumont asked. "I'm not afraid of that phony. I don't care who his friends are. I'll be happy to play along."

"As will I," Froy said. "This Mariutto pretender has no business on the lot."

Paddy topped up their glasses, and they drank on it and everything else they could think of. When our guests finally left, I told Paddy about my run-in with Grove and the story he'd told me about Sugar Stapert, while my boss fussed with the office's venetian blinds. I ended with a pointed question.

"Did Hollywood Security play a part in hushing that up?"

"No," Paddy said as he resumed his seat, "but thanks for asking. What's your interest anyway?"

"If Mariutto was involved in a killing, it could give us more leverage over him than any gas coupons."

"Then again," Paddy said, "reminding him of it could get somebody else killed. We've got our plan. What's more, it's already in motion. What I need now out of you isn't another bright idea. What I need is for you to focus on the task at hand."

CHAPTER THIRTEEN

When I'd told Torrance Beaumont that I'd be babysitting that evening, I hadn't been handing him a line. Long about seven, I was sitting with a sleepy Billy on my knee, watching Ella's face in the lighted mirror of her dressing table. I'd just told her about Max Froy's interest in her latest script. The working title of that was *Private Hopes*, but I was expecting it to change, since Ella was spending an unusual amount of time fussing over what I considered a polished product. In a similar fashion, she was now obsessively arranging and rearranging her long, almost blond hair, though it had looked perfect to me at the end of every round.

We were seated in the master bedroom of our home in Doyle Heights, a 1920s imitation of some of Frank Lloyd Wright's less distinguished work. Ella was preparing to go out, stag, to a retirement dinner for Chester Edson, the man who'd been her boss when she'd worked as a studio publicist. That is, she'd be going out if she could get her hair arranged. At the moment, she was frowning into her mirror. It finally occurred to me that it might be not be over her reflection.

"Was it something I said? You're not bothered by Froy nosing in, are you? I thought you be flattered. And by the way, I didn't bring the subject up with Froy, he brought it up with me."

"I'm not blaming you for that, Scotty. I know who to blame. It's that so-called agent of mine, Mona. She thinks if she starts enough rumors about *Private Hopes* she can touch off a bidding war."

"What's wrong with a little bidding?"

Ella's pale blue eyes narrowed even more, and again I wondered what I'd said. Then she relaxed with an effort.

"Nothing's wrong with it, if the script lives up to the hype. If it doesn't, it will be my reputation that suffers, not Mona's."

"Don't worry about that," I said. And then, when she reached again for her brush, "And leave your hair alone. It's been pinned more often than the Sweetheart of Sigma Chi."

Ella swiveled on her seat to face the two men in her life. She was radiant in a red dress. I decided I should have verified Chester Edson's marital status and maybe his blood pressure.

She said, "I love it when you talk like a B-picture detective. I'll miss that when you outgrow it. That's scheduled to happen when?"

"Not for years and years."

Not many days later, I was summoned from the bullpen where the Hollywood Security operatives rested, when we were given a chance to rest. I found Paddy and Peggy at her desk, both standing.

"The curtain's going up on the next act," Paddy informed me. "Ted Mariutto's due here any minute. He may or may not be accompanied by his shadow—"

"Henchman, you mean," Peggy cut in.

"By his shadow, Al Alsip. Little Al, to his friends. Know either man by sight?"

"No," I said.

"I want you to. Stand behind the bullpen door and open it a crack. You'll be able to observe their entrance. But first go and move that circus wagon you're driving these days. I don't want Mariutto to remember he saw it at our curb."

"Wait a minute. I'm not going to be in the meeting with you?"

"No. If you don't know them, they probably don't know you. That will make your job easier when we get to the tailing part of the operation."

"Operation," Peggy repeated with disdain. "Flea circus is more like it."

"However," Paddy continued with great dignity, "I'd hate for you to miss out on an educational opportunity. So after Mariutto alone or Mariutto and Alsip are safely inside, come back here to Peggy's desk and listen in on the intercom. I'll leave the key down."

"Want us to record it?" Peggy asked. "The Smithsonian might like a copy. For posterity."

"They might at that," Paddy said.

I hurried out to move my car and then reentered the bullpen through its back door. I didn't have a long wait behind the lobby door. I heard Peggy cough, and then two men entered. I'd been picturing Mariutto as a big man, given that his old nickname had been Moose, but the first to stride in, though tall enough, was no bigger around than Jimmy Stewart. He wore his graying brown hair combed straight back like Stewart and a little long, like Stewart had since he'd started making Westerns. At that point, the comparison ran out of gas. The actor had an open, almost boyish face, while Mariutto's was as friendly as the business end of a locomotive, the resemblance to one accentuated by his large, slightly bulbous nose. That cowcatcher accounted for his nickname, I decided.

The second visitor was boyish—not in his face, which was grim, but in his overall dimensions, which were in the Guy De Felice class. Little Al Alsip wore his blond hair in a flattop, adding to the impression that he was the paperboy, here to collect. Or maybe to pick up his date for the prom, as he was wearing an unlikely bow tie and a blue suit that might have been rented, the fit was so bad. Mariutto's sleek gray suit had never been worn by anyone else, if you didn't count his tailor's dummy.

Peggy told them to go right in. Alsip held the right-hand door for his boss and then followed him inside, relieving my mind. There'd always been a chance that he'd have guarded the double doors from the outside, depriving me of my "educational opportunity." As it was, I was seated on the corner of Peggy's desk before the handshaking was out of the way. We leaned into her intercom like it was Sunday night and Jack Benny and Rochester were coming over the Philco.

Mariutto's cultured appearance had led me to expect a voice like Robert Montgomery's, if not Ray Milland's. What I got was more like Howard Keel imitating Bugs Bunny. That is, the voice was as deep as Paddy's, but the accent came from one of New York's less pricey boroughs, I couldn't tell which. Alsip could have sounded like Daffy Duck from all I learned that day; he never spoke.

"Long time no see, Maguire," Mariutto said. "You used to be a regular on the nightclub circuit. Your old ball-and-chain take you in a few links?"

Peggy emitted a sound that might have been a growl. I could plainly hear the smile in Paddy's answer.

"She does feel the loneliness more and more as the years slip by. Of course, we're none of us getting younger. I can't take the nightlife like I used to."

"Right," Mariutto said. "Don't let him fool you, Al. If Maguire starts buying the drinks, hold on to your gold teeth. I remember a night during the war when Morrie Bender tried to squeeze some information out of Maguire concerning a certain union deal Paramount was negotiating. Morrie, who has a hollow leg himself, tried to match him drink for drink and ended up singing 'Sweet Adeline' with some vacationing barbers from Des Moines. Maguire was conducting."

"A happy night," Paddy said.

"A dangerous night," Mariutto said. "It was a lucky thing for you Morrie decided to laugh it off. He's made other citizens very uncomfortable over a lot less trouble than a killer hangover."

At my elbow, Peggy stiffened. I wondered if Mariutto had really been reminiscing or if he'd wanted to remind Paddy of who he had backing him up.

"Speaking of trouble," Paddy said, "what problem can we help you with?"

"A big one," Mariutto said.

I heard Paddy grunt slightly and decided he was reaching across his desk for something. A moment later, he was reading aloud for my benefit and Peggy's.

"Ah, from Washington DC. The Internal Revenue Service. 'Dear Mr. Mariutto.' Da dah, da dah, da dah. 'We have received information regarding undeclared income for the years 1942 through 1945.' Da dah, da dah. 'You will be contacted shortly regarding a possible audit.' Sincerely and so on.

"Dear me. A big problem for certain, but a little out of our line."

"That's not what I hear," Mariutto said. "I hear you saved Tory Beaumont from a tax collector who already had his hand in Beaumont's pocket."

"Someone's been telling tales out of school," Paddy murmured.

"That mean it isn't true?"

"Well, no. We were able to help Tory, but it was a special case. And he's a regular customer of the firm. He uses us for all of his art authentication."

"I'd like you to consider me a regular customer, Maguire. In fact, I insist that you do."

"You may change your mind when you hear what the service set Beaumont back."

"He told me it was plenty, but I couldn't get a round number out of him. Not that it matters. I'll pay a lot to stay out of prison. But how do you bribe a government department?"

"Not the whole department," Paddy said. "Just a local functionary. And don't call it a bribe. Call it a consideration. A certain party approached me a little while back after Hollywood Security played a small part in catching Sidney Shaw's killer. Shaw was a producer, like you, only at RKO. You remember him?"

"No, I don't. What's this party's name?"

"That's for me to know and you not to find out, no matter how curious you get. Not everyone can accept that condition, I know, so if you'd rather call it a day—"

"Go on," Mariutto said.

"For convenience, we can call him the Scarlet Pimpernel, after that guy who rescued people from the guillotine. That's the name we use around here."

"Fine," Mariutto said. "Back to our story."

"As I said, we got a little publicity over the Shaw business. One of the newspaper pieces implied that we weren't above stretching a law or two in the service of a client. A slight exaggeration, but it interested this IRS fellow. He contacted me on the sly and said he could make tax problems go away for a price. He'd been doing it in a small way for years. His technique was to write to Washington to say the matter in question had been resolved. Then he destroyed all local record of it. Bureaucratic inertia did the rest. As far as I know, he still works the same way."

"Why did he need you? You'd just be overhead."

"Because the big risk from the Pimpernel's point of view has been approaching a prospective client. There's always a chance some honest taxpayer will report him or a tax cheat will rat on him in exchange for immunity. With us fronting for him and weeding out the questionable characters, that risk is reduced.

"As for Hollywood Security being overhead, we're not, not for the Pimpernel. We charge a client a referral fee—ten percent of the Pimpernel's own fee—but we never handle the money the client pays him. After we've vetted a client, the Pimpernel collects his fee himself, either in person or through a representative, I've never known which. I'm inclined to think he's farmed the job out, since the collector goes by the name of Smith."

"And how much does this Smith collect?"

"A cool ten thousand."

That was almost three times what the average guy made in a year. I thought Paddy had set the figure too high, but I was forgetting that Mariutto wasn't an average guy.

"I'll pay it," the producer said.

"Hold on a minute," Paddy said. "The money's not the only issue. There's also the pending caseload. The Pimpernel will only take on so many clients a year. He can't risk dozens of files disappearing."

"He's got to risk one more this year, Maguire. Mine. I just got in at Warners. I'm going to make the best movies anybody ever saw, if I have half a chance. I won't be tripped up now."

There was a silence that went on so long Peggy started to reach for the intercom's volume knob. Her bony hand froze in the air when Paddy spoke again.

"All right then. Go get the money ready. And I mean today. Things will happen fast now if they happen at all. This business won't work once a real investigation gets started."

"Thanks, Maguire. I won't forget this."

"I know you won't," Paddy said.

CHAPTER FOURTEEN

I was out of my hiding place and inside Paddy's office within a minute of Mariutto's departure.

"This is never going to work," I said. "When Mariutto's had time to think about this, he's going to see holes inside of holes."

"We're not going to give him time to think," Paddy replied. "This will be like one of those seventy-minute potboilers Max Froy cranked out for Warner Bros. in the good old days. They moved so fast, you never had time to worry about plot holes."

"Okay, what happens when you can't make Mariutto's tax troubles go away because there is no Scarlet Pimpernel?"

"You'll be telling Billy there's no Santa Claus next. Leave the IRS to me. I'll call in an anonymous retraction of my anonymous tip, if I can't think of anything better. Let's not get ahead of ourselves."

"Ahead of ourselves? I can't keep up with ourselves."

Paddy laughed, though in a minor key. "Glad to know you're keeping your sense of humor, Scotty. Now, I have a luncheon appointment with Linda Darnell. She wants us to handle a little problem. For a friend, of course. That is, if you've no other objections."

"One or two. Say we get through this. The day it ends, Mariutto's going to start thinking of ways to cut us out of the tax-fixing racket and himself in. Sooner or later, he's going to figure out there's no racket to hijack."

"You're forgetting he's gone legit."

"His drinking buddies haven't. Suppose one of them gets in trouble with the IRS—that's how they got Capone—and Mariutto sends him our way. Suppose it's Morrie Bender."

"Suppose Dewey beat Truman," Paddy replied with no real interest. "How about we stop supposing and get to work. We have to move fast now, and not just because we have to keep Moose off balance. We don't want a real IRS agent to show up before our man does. I don't expect that to happen; government agencies move slower than Bing Crosby's horses. But we can't take a chance."

"Who are you sending to collect from Mariutto?"

"Someone I can trust to spit in Moose's eye if need be. Or Morrie Bender's, for that matter. A retired cop named Dunne. You met him once, I think."

I had. We'd acquired some inside information from Dunne, and I'd delivered his "consideration." He was as tough as advertised, but also old enough to work a button hook from memory.

"Are you sure he's up to it? I mean, he's, ah . . ."

"Elderly?" Paddy suggested, not laughing now, not even in a minor key.

Paddy had adopted a breezy attitude with Mariutto on the subject of growing older, but I knew it was actually a sore spot for him. Peggy knew about that sore spot, too, and liked to poke it. She'd gotten a kick for years out of describing Paddy as prematurely gray. Lately, she'd been leaving out the "prematurely."

"Dunne's a good man and already coached in his part. Nothing can go wrong there. You hightail it over and relieve Fitzgerald on the Mariutto surveillance. And don't doze off. It would be just like Moose to jump the gun and throw off our whole operation."

Resisting the temptation to steal Peggy's flea circus line, I headed out to retrieve the car I'd hidden away from Mariutto and Alsip. Paddy had called it a "circus wagon," a term he'd used for every car I'd owned since my first day with the agency. He disliked flashy cars, which he thought inappropriate for surveillance work. I thought they blended right in with the normal Hollywood traffic. Besides which, I enjoyed them.

My current ride was a 1951 Hudson Hornet coupe that I considered a compromise between Paddy's tastes and my own.

True, it was long and sleek, with a rounded back end that reminded me of the observation car of a streamliner. But the colors were conservative: dark blue for the roof and pearl gray everywhere else. Everywhere there wasn't chrome, that is. 1951 had been a great year for chrome. Most of the Hornet's was concentrated in its grille, which had two heavy, concentric ovals of chromed steel reinforced by two diagonal bars of it that originated just below Hudson's red emblem, which was itself topped by a rocket-ship hood ornament. Under that hood, my Hornet was a little less modest, as it featured the same dual carburetor setup that Marshall Teague had used to win the Southern 500 at Darlington.

I barely woke those carburetors on the short drive to Wilshire and San Vicente. As I passed the stretch of curb where Fitzgerald sat in his Chevy, I tapped my horn. Then I looked around for a parking space of my own. When I found one that commanded a view of both Mariutto's building and the exit of its parking lot, I squeezed the Hornet into it. A little while later, Fitzgerald cruised by me on his way to lunch.

I relaxed in my seat with my hat brim pulled low, my Luckies on the dash, and an open newspaper propped against the steering wheel. Nothing happened for the first hour and then more nothing happened.

I fell into thinking about the fix we were in. More specifically, I wondered how Paddy would call off the IRS before somebody got hurt. There was always the chance he didn't intend to call them off. He'd said he wanted Mariutto punished for his black marketeering. At this late date, a tax rap might be the only way to do that. But Paddy had also said that the only safe con was one the mark never spotted. If we left Mariutto hanging out to dry, he might realize he'd been set up. Or he might come after us for letting him down.

One possibility remained, as far as I could see. There had to be a real Scarlet Pimpernel. Paddy had never mentioned him before because Paddy was Paddy. And he was using Dunne as a front because he'd spotted the danger of Mariutto trying to cut himself in on the tax-fixing business. Mariutto or Alsip could trail Dunne all day—or try to. The ex-cop would never lead them anywhere important. Once we had whatever evidence Mariutto had collected against Rosa's father, Paddy could place a call to the real Pimpernel and make the IRS problem go away, paying him out of the money Mariutto passed to Dunne.

Working that out calmed me a little. More than that, it gave me a warm glow of self-congratulation. The glow lasted until Hertel, another Hollywood op, came to relieve me. It lasted through a noisy dinner with Billy and a quiet one with Ella. In fact, it lasted until my next shift on the Mariutto watch. That took place after midnight, outside the Sunset Tower, an Art Deco survivor on Sunset Boulevard where the Mariuttos were renting the penthouse. I was again spelling Fitzgerald, a quiet guy from the East Coast whose home address had once been Fenway Park. At least, that was the only home he ever mentioned.

Instead of hurrying off to bed—perhaps at Gilmore Field— Fitzgerald visited me in the Hudson.

"The natives are restless tonight," he said. "Little Al's been doing circuits of the block. He's carrying."

"So am I," I said. I'd brought along my Colt automatic on Paddy's orders. Ella hadn't liked it and then some.

"Okay then," Fitzgerald said.

I sat there in the dark, my earlier worries back with reinforcements. I tried to tell myself that Alsip walking in his sleep did not mean they were on to us. There were plenty of other explanations. He was an insomniac, for all we knew. Or maybe Ted and Rosa had been cutting up rough in the penthouse and Alsip had needed to be elsewhere.

Or he might have felt eyes on him and not known whose they were. I'd been introduced to the feeling in France in 1944 and had felt it often since. Thinking of that phenomenon had the predictable effect: I started to feel watched myself. The sensation got so strong that I found I was spending more time swiveling my head than keeping tabs on the Tower. Finally, I got out of the car and walked to the far end of the block.

It was the kind of night the chamber of commerce would have ordered by the carload if it could have, a perfectly clear and slightly cool night with a million stars overhead and those stars close enough to make the Griffith Park Observatory seem like a waste of money. I told myself that a walk under the stars on a cool night had been all that Alsip had been after. Then I remembered how much like a marionette he'd seemed and called myself a liar.

There was an all-night restaurant across a quiet intersection from the Tower. I moved to its side of the street, crossing well away from the Hornet, and went inside for some nerve tonic. The woman who poured the coffee for me was easily forty, but she hadn't given up the fight. Her hair was a shade of red that most fire departments would have considered excessive. Her big eyes, very big for that hour of the morning, were looking me over closely.

"Didn't you used to be in the movies?" she asked.

It was a question I didn't mind hearing, normally. But at that moment, I caught a moving reflection in the dark glass of the display case behind the waitress. Little Al Alsip had entered the restaurant behind me and was walking toward the counter where I stood. He was carrying either a big gun or a small toaster under the jacket of his boys-department suit.

I said, "Funny. I was just going to ask if you'd been in pictures."

That long shot paid off for me. The waitress launched into a recap of her appearances in several Busby Berkeley musicals, starting with the featured turn she'd had in the opening number of *Gold Diggers of 1933*, "We're in the Money." As she talked, Alsip arrived at the counter and put a crumpled dollar bill on it. That must have been a regular occurrence, because the former dancer replaced the bill with quarters without taking her eyes from mine. I was careful not to break eye contact either, not until Alsip had taken his coins and shambled to the cigarette machine near the exit. He used both the machine and the door without a backward glance at me.

I used them both myself, after tipping the waitress so much she may have considered us engaged. Then I went back to my car, taking the long way again. "We're in the Money" was playing in my head. I hadn't believed the lyrics in 1933 and I didn't believe them now.

CHAPTER FIFTEEN

After my midnight surveillance shift, I'd intended to sleep till noon the next day. I barely made it to nine. That was when Ella dropped by to say that Paddy was on the line and unhappy.

"It's Dunne," Paddy said after I'd mumbled my name into the nearest phone. "He died in his sleep last night. I just spoke to his wife. Widow, I mean. He was due to see Mariutto later this morning. Pick me up on your way in. We'll discuss it over breakfast."

We ate at the counter of Schwab's Pharmacy, which wasn't many blocks from the Sunset Tower. I kept watching for Little Al Alsip over my shoulder, and that took away from Paddy's enjoyment of his "Number Five," flannel cakes and bacon.

"Relax and eat," he said. "We've a long day ahead of us. The first order of business is deciding whether we ask for a postponement or try to find someone else to brace Moose. If we push back the meeting, it'll give Moose more time to spot those plot holes you were worrying over yesterday. More time to regain his balance in general, when what we want is to keep him teetering."

Mariutto hadn't seemed particularly off balance to me or even edgy. Alsip had, though, and he might have caught it from his boss.

"I say we go ahead," I said.

"Okay, so who takes Dunne's place? We may have to use one of our own people. Lange might've gotten away with it—he's nearly as tough as Dunne—but he's on assignment in Reno."

"There's me," I said.

Paddy almost dropped the maple syrup. "You? Don't get me wrong, Scotty, there's no one under Peggy on the cast list who I trust more than you. But I doubt even Billy thinks of you as a hard case. And speaking of Billy, you might remember him and Ella before you volunteer to go lion taming."

"How does lion taming even enter into it? We're not planning a stickup. This is an acting job. And I used to be an actor."

"How'd that work out for you?"

I conceded the point by shifting my attack. "And where's the danger? I'll be picking up money from a guy who's anxious to hand it over. I'll barely have to get out of my car."

"It may involve a little more than that," Paddy said.

Even so, I was pretty sure I had him. He was staring at a rack of soda glasses behind the counter and tapping his coffee cup with a piece of bacon.

"You sure you've had no dealings with Mariutto?" he finally asked.

"Positive." I then remembered my near encounter with Al Alsip only a few hours earlier. I started to mention it, but Paddy spoke first.

"You may run into Moose after this, and he may remember you then. That could be a problem. We could fit you out with a pair of windowpane eyeglasses today and part your hair differently. That greasepaint and the passage of time might cover you going forward."

The idea of wearing a disguise tabled my unspoken concerns about Little Al. He couldn't have gotten that good a look at me while he'd been breaking his dollar—if he'd noticed me at all. Eyeglasses would make it that much safer.

Paddy bit off the end the bacon slice he'd been using to keep time. "We'll try it," he said. "Finish up and let's go."

I made an effort, but I was suddenly having a hard time swallowing. Driving turned out to be a challenge, too, due to a wandering mind. Paddy noticed and gave me more helpful advice than usual. When he suddenly told me to pull into a lot we were passing, I thought he was taking me out of the game. Then I saw that the lot belonged to Golden State Car Rental.

"Mariutto may or may not have noticed this painted Jezebel of yours following him around, but he's certain to know the make and model of whatever car you drive today because he'll have you followed when you leave him. They know me here, and they won't mind me signing Smith on the rental agreement. That's the name Mariutto will be expecting, if he traces the car this far. Pick yourself out something nice."

I took Paddy at his word and selected a 1951 Chrysler Saratoga with the new hemi V-8. If Alsip tried to follow me in that, he'd better be wearing his Keds.

Back at the office, Paddy told Peggy to report with a comb and a mirror, and the two of them spent a quarter hour playing with my hair, Paddy supervising and Peggy working the comb. She grew so grim over it that I thought she'd found a bald spot. They finally selected a high part, just off the centerline, that made me look like I'd picked my style in 1935 and married it. Whether it made me look like a rogue accountant was another matter.

Next they tried phony eyeglasses on me, finally choosing a pair whose frames were so heavy and black they were bound to be the first thing anyone noticed and the last thing anyone forgot.

Only then did Peggy speak up. "This idea is daft. Call Central Casting and hire somebody."

"Out," Paddy said. "And hold my calls. I'll be coaching Scotty in his part. And don't you be calling Ella and worrying her for no good reason. We've made up our mind. Mind singular, because I'm using the royal we."

"You give me a pain," Peggy replied. "Also royal."

When the office doors slammed together, Paddy swiveled in his chair and rooted in the credenza behind his desk. He came up with a leather briefcase, which he winged across the desk to me.

"Dunne supplied his own props, God rest him," Paddy said, "but that should serve just as well."

"To carry the money out?"

"And Mariutto's tax records in. You'll remember me asking De Felice for as many tax returns as he could find and photograph." Paddy produced a thick manila folder. "The little roach came through for us; I'll say that for him. These are your bona fides. If Moose doesn't hand you his money as fast as you seem to think he's going to, I want you to make a show of going through these under his watchful eye, so he'll believe you really are on the inside.

"You might even want to spread them out on his desk, so he'll get a good look. All the time, be telling him that things are serious but not hopeless. The way I wove the tale, Moose isn't sure who he'll be receiving, the Scarlet Pimpernel or a flunky. That should cover any flubs you make. When he's had an eyeful, put everything away. By then, he should have handed over the ten grand and maybe thrown in a tip."

"And if he hasn't?"

"Then you'll have to ask him for it. If he holds out or tries to dicker, get up and leave. Ditto if he starts asking questions. Now let's go through the business a couple of times, without the patter first and then with it."

I did as ordered, and it was a good thing I rehearsed. Paddy's briefcase was an older design with straps that buckled like a belt and a locking tongue. Neither buckles nor lock had been worked recently, though they loosened up a little more with each pass. I did myself.

Then, during my fourth run-through, Paddy stopped me just as I got the tax returns spread out on his desk.

"I suppose you know all about gas rationing," he said.

"Only what I read in *Stars and Stripes.*"

"We've a few minutes to kill. I'll give you a primer. As I recall, gas rationing didn't get going until the end of '42. You were in uniform how long by then?"

"I was drafted before Pearl Harbor, lucky guy that I am."

"You were lucky you missed rationing at least. It was run by the Office of Price Administration and was therefore a bureaucrat's idea of heaven: committees, boards, forms, coupons, points, and miles of red tape. For gas, you are issued coupons by the local OPA board that got you so many gallons a week, based on your occupation or pull. They ranged from four gallons a week for 'A' coupons up to all you wanted for 'X' coupons. Those went to Congressmen. Also to the Goldwyn Girls.

"Naturally a black market sprang up, courtesy of free spirits like Moose Mariutto. As I think I told you, they started with stolen coupons—the OPA lost one sheet for every ten it printed—and moved on to counterfeits, like the ones Moose claims to have stashed away."

Paddy had been lecturing with his chair tilted back and his cigar held above his head. Now he sat up straight and opened the center drawer of his desk.

"I forgot I had these when we were discussing coupons with De Felice the other day. I took them off a certain MGM choreographer I bailed out after he'd been nabbed driving drunk. He'd hid these in his shirt, as they were counterfeits. Maybe Moose's own."

He handed me a sheet of perforated coupons, each containing a prominent letter "A." A small number appeared beside the letter, a different number for each row. Each coupon also had a tiny space for writing in the license number and registration of a car.

"Why counterfeit 'A' stamps?" I asked. "Isn't that like counterfeiting one dollar bills? Why not go for the 'X' stamps? Oh right, the windshield stickers."

"Exactly. The coupon you handed over to the gas pump jockey had to correspond to the windshield sticker you'd been issued for your car. I'm surprised you even know about those. You soldiers certainly lived the carefree life. Unlimited food, unlimited gas—"

"Unlimited small arms fire," I said, tossing the coupon sheet onto Paddy's desk.

"Speaking of which," he said. "Where's your gun?"

"In the glove compartment of the Saratoga. I moved it over from my car while you were giving the rental clerk a false name."

"Leave the holster there. Put the Colt in the bag."

"Is that in character?"

"Forget your acting classes. The gun may come in handy if things go to blazes." He opened his desk drawer again, this time producing a map and a camera. "If things go well, here's what I want you to do next."

He gave me my final instructions with one eye on his watch. When he'd finished, he said, "Good luck. Peggy's outside, waiting to kiss you good-bye."

CHAPTER SIXTEEN

Paddy had told me to park as close to Mariutto's building as I could, so I selected a visitor space in its own little lot. I parked in that space awkwardly, perhaps because the Saratoga had the same turning radius as its aircraft carrier namesake, perhaps because my palms were sweating.

I told myself that my jitters weren't over Mariutto being an ex-racketeer with mob connections but because this was an acting job, as I'd told Paddy at Schwab's. In my acting days, I'd always been nervous before the cameras started to roll and fine once they did. Back then, my nerves had been calmed by the concentration film acting required. You couldn't do it if you couldn't forget the camera and lights and booms and the people behind them. But once you did, it was just you and the other actors and a scene that went exactly as you'd rehearsed it. That was how it had been then, and that was how it would be today.

Ted Mariutto Productions occupied a suite on the second floor of a small but very modern building, its lobby paneled in pitted, matte-finished stone, its elevators clad in a dull brass that was stamped with a geometric pattern. The stamping kept the golden doors from displaying my reflection, but my altered image ambushed me on the second floor, in the glass front of the Mariutto suite. I didn't recognize myself at first, and that was encouraging. So was the modest crowd in the waiting room beyond the glass. If I'd been expecting to pay off a crooked official, I'd have cleared out the witnesses. Not Moose, who may have bribed three in an average day. I told myself that this was going to be as fast and routine as I'd assured Paddy.

The waiting room was under the command of a raven-haired woman seated behind a centrally placed desk. She was wearing a turquoise dress covered with white polka dots and an expression that dared me to comment on them. The nameplate on her desk was big enough to be a producer's and bore a name that would have suited one: Helen Gallimore.

"Yes?" she said like it was a word she didn't enjoy using.

"Mr. Smith to see Mr. Mariutto."

She keyed her intercom, gave my alias, and nodded me toward the door behind her so efficiently that I wished I had commented on her polka dots just to give me time to catch my breath.

I lost what air I carried when I noticed who was guarding the door to the inner office. It was Al Alsip. He'd blended in with the waiting room crowd because he'd been seated with his face behind a copy of *True Detective*. As I approached, he lowered the magazine and studied me. There was no sign of recognition in his beady eyes, just the sincere desire to know me the next time he saw me.

Before I could settle down, I was seated in Mariutto's office, getting a full view of a face I'd only seen in profile. For anyone who'd hung around the movie business as long as I had, it was hard to look at an unfamiliar face without wondering how well it would photograph. My guess was that Mariutto would have flunked his screen test. It wasn't the thick nose—any number of actors and even a few actresses had gotten by with those. It was that the head the nose went with was too thin, by which I mean narrow. That put the hooded brown eyes too close together and squeezed the small mouth. Mariutto compensated for the latter problem by keeping one corner of his mouth cocked upward in a perpetual smirk.

"So you're the guy who's going to get me off the hook," he said.

"We certainly intend to," I said, trying to make the "we" sound anything but royal. I was also affecting an accent, another layer for my all too see-through disguise. My choice was a Hoosier twang, which I could do in my sleep and, according to Ella, sometimes did.

"For a consideration, of course," I added.

"Of course," Mariutto said, but without reaching for any bags with dollar signs on them.

I reached for my own bag then and attacked the first stiff buckle. Lifting the bag and feeling its weight reminded me of the gun inside and that reminded me of the possibility of a hasty exit. I glanced around for a back door and spotted one.

"Your case is not that unusual," I said as I scanned the rest of the room. "The late war left a lot of people's tax histories with, ah, gray areas. That works to our advantage."

"What's one more tree in a forest?" Mariutto said.

"Exactly."

His office wasn't as big as Paddy's but it had more windows, though the view was largely other buildings and the lower fronds of palm trees. Surprisingly, the desk was also modest, in size and decoration. There was no brass nameplate or any trophy knickknacks, only a small stack of what I took for movie scripts. It wasn't the desk of a pretender, the term Max Froy had used for our mark. I decided Mariutto had told my boss the truth. He really intended to make good in his new job.

I'd negotiated the briefcase buckles and was struggling with its tongue, while my own babbled on. "It's almost always a question of evidence. Any citizen can report another for tax, ah, irregularities, but how many can produce supporting evidence? In the absence of that, a negative report from the field office is always accepted."

"A negative report meaning a positive report, from my point of view," Mariutto said.

"Exactly."

The tongue popped open just before I asked my host for the loan of a knife. So far, I've been following the line of patter Paddy had laid out, but I was running out of script pages fast.

"Based on the photostatic copies we were sent, your tax returns themselves contain no obvious red flags."

I pulled out the prop folder and opened it on the desk. "I believe we have everything going back to 1940," I said. Then the bottom fell out.

I'd been turning the forms over one by one. And stuck between the 1942 return and the one for 1943 was the sheet of counterfeit gas coupons Paddy had shown me. Somehow I must have shuffled it in with my papers before I'd set out.

I covered the sheet quickly, closed the folder, and got it back inside the briefcase on my second try. All the while, I kept talking.

"It's really just a matter of us sending that negative report before a field agent is assigned to your file and starts a, ah, real investigation."

I finally stole a glance at Mariutto. He hadn't reacted at all, except that his smirk was gone. Without taking his eyes from mine, he pulled open the right-hand drawer of his desk and reached inside. My right hand, still inside the briefcase, closed around the butt of my forty-five.

I didn't draw the gun when Mariutto withdrew his hand because his movement was accompanied by the sound of protesting paper. His hand came out holding a fat manila envelope, which he tossed onto his desk.

"We'd better get a move on then," he said.

CHAPTER SEVENTEEN

As I stepped back into the Ted Mariutto Productions waiting room, I checked Little Al Alsip's seat by the door. It was empty. I glanced around for him and spotted my own reflection again. That is, I thought for a split second I was again seeing myself in the suite's plate glass outer wall. It was actually a man standing at Helen Gallimore's desk. He was tall and dark like me, wore a dated hairstyle and a nondescript suit like me, and was peering at Gallimore's polka dots through dark-framed eyeglasses, as I'd done not many minutes earlier.

I stepped up behind Gallimore as the newcomer said, "Conover, Internal Revenue Service, to see Mr. Mariutto. And no, I don't have an appointment."

So much for how slow government agencies moved. I hurried around the desk, trying to figure a way to keep the con alive.

"Mr. Mariutto's left by his private entrance," I said to Gallimore. "He asked me to tell you he'll be gone the rest of the day."

That was a risk and a half, since the back door I'd seen in Mariutto's office might have belonged to a bathroom or closet. I was counting on Gallimore backing me up just to give her boss a breather. She didn't. After a confused glance at me, then Conover, then me again, Gallimore pushed the buzzer on her intercom. Everyone in the waiting room sat up. And no one answered.

"Mr. Mariutto," Gallimore said into the box. "Mr. Mariutto?"

My heart rate started to drop back to double digits.

Then Conover said, "Permit me." He brushed past me and strode around the desk.

Gallimore jumped up, too late to block him. I was moving in the opposite direction, for the glass exit. I reached it just as Conover threw open the door to Mariutto's sanctuary. A collective sigh went up from the hopefuls in the waiting room. The office was unoccupied.

By then I was heading for the stairs. I didn't want to chance riding down in the elevator with my double. Not with a ten-thousand-dollar payoff in my possession. I made a mental note to apologize to Paddy later. Evidently the IRS did employ hard cases for their fieldwork.

While I was at it, I'd complement Paddy on the foresight he'd shown when he'd given me detailed instructions for the rest of my day. Without them, I would have driven straight to the nearest cocktail lounge. As it was, I was heading east on Wilshire within two minutes of hitting the fire stairs. But not alone. As I'd pulled into traffic, a Pontiac Chieftain had fallen in behind me.

I was almost downtown when I reached my next stop, another office building, taller than Mariutto's, though older. Old enough, in fact, to still employ elevator operators. After a cursory glance at the building's directory, I asked the little man who was holding a car for me for De Felice Investigations.

"Fourth floor," he told me.

That confirmed the directory. I'd only asked for the benefit of the guy who'd driven the Chieftain and then tailed me on foot into the lobby: Al Alsip. He didn't join me in the elevator, but I knew he'd be counting the minutes till I returned.

De Felice's secretary could have given Helen Gallimore lessons in saying hello. Also in smiling. The young woman, whose name I never caught, had plenty to smile about, from what I could see of her. That viewing was all too short, as I was once again denied a moment to cool my heels.

De Felice called to me from his office door and showed me inside like an usher who worked for tips. That wasn't surprising, given what I carried. What was surprising was the name he called me.

"Thomas, my good friend. It is marvelous to see you, even in those extravagant eyeglasses."

Thomas was my real first name, which I'd given up at Paramount's insistence when I'd signed my first contract.

"Come again?"

"Forgive the familiarity, Thomas. I didn't think you would mind, now that we're comrades in arms. I must say the name fits you much better than Scotty. You are a doubter by nature, are you not? You did not believe our current enterprise would work, and yet here you are."

"Mrs. Mariutto isn't divorced yet."

"A mere detail."

It probably was for De Felice. Certainly it couldn't compare in importance to what I'd brought him in my prop briefcase. I opened it now—with no trouble at all—and took out the yellow envelope. It would have served us both right if it had contained cut-up newspaper, but it didn't. The various denominations were still in their paper straps. I tossed bundles and loose bills amounting to three thousand, three hundred, and thirty-three dollars onto De Felice's big Hollywood blond desk. Then I looked on as the private inquiry agent removed each strap and counted each bundle in turn.

"Satisfied?" I said when he'd finished.

"There's still a matter of my thirty-three cents. I am joking, Thomas. Do not be so serious. You must learn to face danger with a light heart."

"Speaking of danger," I said. "Paddy's worried that we might be heading into some."

"Surely we have been in some from the start."

"Not all three of us this time. Just Paddy and me."

"I do not understand."

"Paddy's afraid that, sooner or later, you'll decide to rat us out to Mariutto."

"Thomas, why would I? And I resent the word 'rat.' It is uncouth in the extreme."

"Sorry, I was quoting Paddy. He has his uncouth moments. As to why you would, it'd be for another payday like this one, from Mariutto or from us, if you decide you have something you can hold over our heads. All because you feel safe right now. Mariutto's been to see Paddy over this, and I've been to see him. You might feel like we're handcuffed to this deal and you're not. Turns out I was followed here by one of Mariutto's boys."

De Felice's little moustache twitched.

"So you're handcuffed now, yourself. If Moose ever finds out he was conned, we'll all end up against the same wall."

I had to hand it to De Felice. Apart from that moustache tell, he didn't flinch.

"I will be honored to have your company, Thomas, my friend," he said.

The De Felice part of the program hadn't proven as satisfying as I'd expected, but I still had high hopes for the next item on the agenda: losing my shadow. I'd told Paddy that the easiest way to do it would be to walk out the back door of De Felice's building and hail a cab. The car rental people could pick up the Chrysler at their leisure. He'd rejected the idea, saying that he wanted Alsip occupied for another half hour at least.

So I headed back west on Wilshire. I'd driven like my grandmother on the way east to De Felice's and I stuck to the same system now. That lulled Alsip into hanging well back.

My method of shaking a tail, learned from watching too many movies, was to risk my own neck and everyone else's with some high-speed driving. Paddy's technique, learned from watching too much baseball, was to slow everything down to a walk. Eventually, the tail would become bored and careless. Today we were using the Maguire method.

The map Paddy had given me during my briefing was one many visitors to LA took home with them: a map to the movie stars' homes. I had it open on the seat beside me. When we reached the southern half of Beverly Hills, I left the boulevard. Our first stop was the home of Louella Parsons on Maple Drive. Once there, I got out of my car, checked my watch, and took a photograph with the camera Paddy had given me. Alsip watched from the corner of Carmelita Avenue.

I stayed on Maple until I came to the George Burns and Gracie Allen house, where I repeated the exact procedure, wristwatch check and all. Then I cut over to Crescent, to a mansion belonging to the director Vincent Minnelli, according to Paddy. It must have been a recent acquisition, because it was only marked in pencil on my map. Then I visited Lupe Velez's old place on Rodeo Drive and Marlene Dietrich's Art Deco pile on Roxbury. By then I would have had the start of a nice little souvenir album, if Paddy had given me any film. I was also well on my way to putting Alsip to sleep, I hoped.

I'd pulled onto Roxbury from Sunset, and Alsip had followed me, parking just past the corner. Now I did something I hadn't done once during our tour. I turned around in a driveway, Dietrich's, in fact. That handed Alsip a small problem. He had to turn around himself, but he couldn't do it until I passed him. It was only a small problem because I was still inching along in low gear. At least I was until I came abreast of Alsip's Pontiac. Then I took off like a startled drag racer.

I made the right onto Sunset without even tapping my brakes and then turned right again onto Bedford. I stayed on Bedford all the way down to Santa Monica Boulevard. If I was guessing right, by then Alsip was speeding east on Sunset. And swearing.

CHAPTER EIGHTEEN

I drove to the Golden State Car Rental lot by a route that, drawn on a map, would have looked like an electrocardiogram of a minor heart attack. The Saratoga had gone from being an asset to a serious liability, and I happily traded it for my waiting Hornet. At the same time, I took off the Clark Kent glasses—for good, I hoped—and put on my holster, filling it from the briefcase before I locked that in my trunk.

Next, I drove to a little lunch wagon that was just big enough to have a phone. The place was called Mike's, and it was more or less a Hollywood Security branch office. Our operatives used it to drop off messages for one another and to phone in, when there wasn't time to drive back to Roe Street. The braver operatives also ate there. I was thinking of a hamburger with onions and figuring I'd earned it. I was wrong.

As soon as I stepped through the door, Rene, the bird lover who worked behind the counter, pointed to the wall phone. Sighing all the way, I crossed to it and called Peggy Maguire.

"Scotty, good. Paddy needs you in San Pedro. Do you know where that is?"

"On the road to Mandalay, isn't it? An hour okay?"

"This very minute would be two minutes late." She gave me directions that contained no kiss good-bye. Even so, Peggy was looking out for me. As I passed the counter, Rene handed me a paper sack of ham sandwiches she'd had ready and waiting.

San Pedro actually was on the road to Mandalay. That is to say, if you walked a line between downtown Los Angeles and the Far East, San Pedro would be the last place you'd have dry feet. It was squeezed between the Palos Verdes Peninsula, the southernmost terminus of Santa Monica Bay, and sprawling Long Beach.

Peggy's directions took me to the San Pedro Swim Club. Rocking on his heels in its parking lot was her husband. Paddy tore into what I'd left of the sandwiches while I gave him my report, his chewing slowing while I described how I'd accidentally displayed the counterfeit gas coupons and coming to a complete stop when I mentioned Conover of the IRS showing up just too late to gum our play.

"We were right to go ahead today" was Paddy's only comment until I got to my time in Beverly Hills. Then he chuckled.

"Having you check your watch at every stop was the beauty part," he said. "Alsip is still trying to figure that out.

"Here's how I spent my lunch hour. When Moose bolted following your interview, Hertel and I were ready and waiting. He led us straight out here, to an old fire trap on the coast road. During the war, it was a roadhouse called the Sea Hawk. The customers were an oil-and-water mix of ship workers from Long Beach and Hollywood types looking for a quiet place to woo other people's spouses. Moose was inside for ten minutes. He left empty-handed and Hertel followed him, stopping here long enough to drop me off. He's studying law at night, did you know that?"

"Mariutto?"

"Hertel."

"What did Mariutto do at the Sea Hawk?"

"You and I are about to find out."

It was a short drive to the roadhouse, but long enough for me to incur my employer's displeasure.

Paddy set me up by saying, "I'd always heard the Sea Hawk was owned by Errol Flynn. I never knew he had Moose Mariutto as a silent partner."

"According to Sergeant Grove," I said, "Sugar Stapert, the singer Mariutto may have killed, was shot in a roadhouse. It's got to be the same place."

"According to Patrick J. Maguire," Paddy said, "you're

supposed to be focusing on the task at hand. If anyone holding out a blank check comes to you about this Stapert canary, let me know. Otherwise, forget the name.

"Ours is the next turning on the right."

It belonged to a big frame house, maybe seventy years old, standing on its own semicircle of seaside cliff. We parked in a weedy gravel lot that must have been a remnant of the property's night club days. Others were awning frames above the lower story windows and the front door that now only supported tatters of striped cloth and a rusted metal box on one corner of the house that might once have held the works of a neon sign.

"I'm surprised even the Pacific could do this much damage in only ten years," Paddy observed. "Something about this setup is making me think of Abbott and Costello, though I'm not sure why."

"*Hold That Ghost*," I said. "Abbott and Costello inherit a defunct roadhouse from a dead gangster. Named Moose."

Paddy grinned. "I'm going to get you on *Quiz Kids* if it's the last thing I do. I wonder if our Moose took his nickname from that movie or if some brave screenwriter stole it from him. He used the back door, by the way."

That door was small and metal and totally without rust. The brass of the lock was bright.

"Guy De Felice fancies himself a housebreaker," Paddy said, pocketing the flashlight he'd taken from my glove compartment. "Let's see how I compare."

He had the door open before I could place my bet. The inside of the Sea Hawk was like a time capsule. The kitchen, the room we entered, was in perfect order, if you overlooked the dust. The neighboring bar had been stripped of bottles but not glassware. Beyond it, in the club's main room, the tables had tablecloths and the windows curtains, all gray with the same dust that covered the plates and pots in the kitchen.

"Smell smoke?" I asked.

"Been smelling it."

The room had a big fireplace, left over from the days when the house had been a house. On its hearth was a pile of feathery ashes around a core of dying embers.

"So much for Moose's gas stamp hoard," Paddy said. "We've

drawn out his trumps, now we have to win the hand or it's all been for nothing. By that I mean we have to find Moose's hidey hole. Toward that end, I'd like to call your attention to a strange feature of the housekeeping in this place."

"There hasn't been any housekeeping, not for years."

"That so? Look down at your feet."

I did. The wooden floor gleamed in what light there was. "Someone swept the floors."

"Someone's kept them swept, you mean. Ever since Moose got back from Omaha, probably. The haunted house business is a perfect disguise for Moose's Fort Knox. But he couldn't take the chance of anyone tracking his footsteps. Still, the sweeping may tell us something. Go check the second floor. The floor of the second floor, to be exact."

I did. The upstairs hallway and the stairs leading up to it were both carpeted with dust. I reported that to Paddy, whom I found in a room identified as the manager's office. He was standing next to an open wall safe.

"Fast work," I said.

"Not by me. It was standing open. Has been since the place closed, from the looks of it. No sweeping upstairs? Good. That limits our search to this floor."

"How about the basement?"

"I checked it while you were mountaineering. You could grow tomatoes on the basement steps."

I glanced around the paneled room and saw something I should have seen the moment I'd entered. It had big, doleful eyes and even bigger antlers.

Paddy had followed my gaze. "Right," he said, "a moose head. Mariutto's claim to ownership of the club, for anyone bright enough to figure out his joke."

"And maybe a nod to *Hold That Ghost*," I said.

"If you're about to tell me that Costello found the dead gangster's money inside a moose head so we should look for Mariutto's blackmail papers inside that thing, I'll have a breakdown."

"The other feature of the roadhouse in the movie was hidden gambling equipment. Some of it was behind sliding panels."

"Now you're talking," Paddy said. "What we need is a windowless wall in a room whose measurements aren't the same inside as out. We might as well start with this room, since the moose is in here, egging us on."

He rapped the wall to the left of the door with my flashlight. "This wall backs onto the bar. Go out and pace it off from the bar side."

"Fifteen feet," I said when I returned.

"It's not fifteen in here."

I checked it. "Twelve."

Paddy turned to face the moose. "So our sad friend is hanging three feet closer to us than he should be. Start pressing knots in the knotty pine."

We checked the wall, panel by panel. The spring release wasn't a knot. It was a nail from which a photo of a schooner, Errol Flynn's own *Zaca*, hung. When Paddy pushed the nail in, the nearest panel slipped back like it had been oiled yesterday.

Behind it was an ordinary closet with unfinished pine shelves. The bottom two shelves were empty. The rest held a miscellaneous collection of shoeboxes, bundles of paper tied with ribbon or string, and envelopes.

"Hear that?" Paddy asked.

"Just the house settling," I said.

"This house finished settling before you were born," Paddy said. "Go look."

I hesitated, afraid to leave my boss alone with all that blackmail fodder. Then a board creaked, maybe in the kitchen, and I went out, gun in hand.

I didn't find anything to shoot, not even an uncouth rat, but then I only got a minute or two to search before Paddy whistled me back. He was holding a long white envelope.

"What was Rosa's father's name again?"

"George Yowell."

"Check," he said. "Mission accomplished. Remember what De Felice said? 'I was asked to do the extraordinary and I did it extraordinarily well.' Ought to be on our business cards."

He placed the envelope in an inside breast pocket of his suit coat. As far as I could tell, he hadn't stuffed the others while I'd been out ghost hunting.

"Won't Mariutto miss that?"

"No. He'll be too busy missing the whole place. We're going to burn it down. For our peace of mind, Moose can never know he was conned, remember."

"Burning down the building won't tip him off?"

"No. He'll think he did it himself when he torched those counterfeit coupons. Bring me a couple of the fatter bundles, and leave the panel open. We want that stuff to burn if nothing else does. That'll keep Moose out of mischief for a while."

I selected the bundles and followed Paddy into the main room. He was fanning the embers from the coupon bonfire with his homburg.

"I have a match," I said.

"So do I. This is more poetic. Hold a fistful of paper down here. Good. Hand me another and go light some curtains."

We drove out by way of Portuguese Bend, stopping on a little rise to examine our handiwork. The Sea Hawk was burning like King Kong's gate, fanned by a land breeze that was sending a long trail of black smoke out to sea.

"We just destroyed the Sugar Stapert crime scene," I said. "Sergeant Grove is not going to be happy."

"When has he ever been?" Paddy asked.

CHAPTER NINETEEN

I was hoping Paddy would bring in Rosa Mariutto yet that day, since
we now had the IRS breathing down our necks. The sooner we
called them off, if they could be called off, the better I'd sleep.
Paddy might have been thinking the same thing, because he used
the prearranged signal—set up in case Mariutto was having his
wife's phone calls monitored—as soon as we got back to Roe
Street.

Peggy placed the actual call to the Mariutto penthouse. She
asked for Musso and Frank's Grill, got huffy with whoever told her
she'd gotten a wrong number, and hung up. Thirty minutes later,
Rosa called back from a phone booth. The earliest she could meet
us was the next morning, which satisfied Paddy. He gave me the
rest of the day off, which satisfied me. Especially after I got home
and found Ella happier than she'd been in weeks. She'd finished
Private Hopes for the last time and was ready to celebrate. As it
turned out, I had no trouble sleeping that night whatsoever.

Rosa reported, sans Guy De Felice, the next morning, wearing a
beige linen suit and another of her broad-brimmed hats. It put her
eyes in shadow again, but I was still able to spot the glint in them
when Paddy produced the white envelope bearing her father's name.

"I took the precaution of looking these over," he said. "They're
records of under-the-table beef sales George Yowell made during
the war and an affidavit from one of the middlemen he dealt with,
now conveniently dead."

Rosa took the envelope and examined each folded sheet with care. "Now what?"

"Now," Paddy said, "if you'll be guided by me, we burn them. We would have done it yesterday, but I wanted you to be sure that your husband's hold on you is well and truly broken."

"I could mail them to Daddy."

"And they could miscarry. In fact, walking out of here with them in your possession is a risk. And not just for you."

"I followed your instructions coming over. I changed cabs twice."

"Even so."

Rosa thought about it for as long as it took her to cross, uncross, and recross her long legs.

"Burn them," she said.

"Scotty, if you'll do the honors."

Paddy's office lacked a fireplace. We made do with a metal trashcan and an open window. While the papers burned, Paddy discussed the future.

"On the subject of our mutual safety," he said, "I'd like you to hold off filing for your divorce for a while. I don't want Moose to connect the filing with our little business deal."

"How long are we talking about?"

"Just until he strays again."

"That won't be a hardship."

"Good. When that happens, you can call it the straw that broke the camel's back, if that doesn't sound too personal. If Moose mentions black-market beef, never let on that you know he's bluffing. Tell him your father has offered to sacrifice himself for your happiness. You'll be a free woman in no time."

Rosa kissed Paddy good-bye shortly afterward. "Too bad you're married," she said. But when she said it, she winked at me.

After she'd gone, Paddy whistled. "There goes temptation on the hoof. Luckily, she won't be single long. I see an oilman in her future."

"I see a taxman in our future. Name of Conover. He's probably in with Mariutto right now."

Paddy's reply was interrupted by the buzz of the intercom, followed by a tinny reproduction of Peggy's voice. "A gentleman from the IRS to see you."

"You were saying," Paddy said to me before addressing the box. "Send him in."

Conover of the IRS entered. I stood up, hoping to be dismissed, but Paddy waved me back to my seat. Then he produced the office bottle of Irish whiskey and three glasses. To Conover, he said, "Too early for you?"

"Not familiar with the concept," Conover replied. He tossed his briefcase onto Paddy's desk, the thud of its landing making me jump. At the same time, he removed his heavy eyeglasses. Those he carefully placed on the briefcase.

"Philip," Paddy said as he poured, "this is Scotty, my top operative. Scotty, now that Phil has dropped the Conover disguise, does he look familiar?"

The ex-Conover gave me full face and profile. At close range, he looked a little like a retired pug—his brow and the bridge of his nose were both scarred—but not one I could remember ever seeing in the ring.

"Well," Paddy said, "it has been ten years and more, with an army hitch thrown in for good measure. Phil was mixed up in that business you poked your nose into before the war, the Owen Taylor case. He's what the pulps call a private dick. After that long lost evening when you and I visited Lido Pier, I made a point of meeting him. I've used him more than once since on especially sensitive matters."

The private eye raised his glass to Paddy, drained it, and said, "Sorry to drink and run, but . . ."

"I understand," Paddy said. He handed our visitor a familiar looking pay packet and walked him to the office's double doors.

I waited until Paddy was back and comfortably settled in his chair. Then I said, "Out with it."

"It?"

"You sent a private detective to Mariutto's office to pose as an IRS agent when you knew I'd be there posing as an IRS agent. Why?"

"Ah, that it." Paddy produced and lit a cigar, sliding his ashtray over to serve us both. "There were two reasons for that. The first was to turn up the heat under the pot. I'd told Moose that the real danger for him was an IRS investigation getting started before our

Scarlet Pimpernel phantasm could quash it. You repeated the same warning to him yesterday, if you followed my prompts. Having 'Agent Conover' show up was intended to nudge Moose off the fence. It turned out no nudging was needed.

"My second reason for sending Phil in was also worry wasted, since you made it out of Moose's office under your own steam. If for any reason you hadn't, he was to get you out."

I shook a Lucky from my pack but didn't get it to my lips before a glimmer of dawn poked me between the eyes. "Why didn't you just send this Phil character in Dunne's place?"

"He could never have pulled off the job you did, Scotty. I wish I could've seen your face when you turned up that sheet of gas coupons. If it hadn't been a second-floor office, I would've been peeking in the window."

I'd gotten my lighter going, but it didn't reach my cigarette. "Wait a minute. Are you saying I didn't pick up those coupons by mistake? Are you saying you somehow slipped them into my folder without me noticing? I don't believe it."

"You've seen me pull a dime out of Billy's ear, haven't you? Do you think they really grow in there?"

"But why?"

"As I tried to impress on you and De Felice that first day, motivating Moose was job number one. We couldn't afford to sit around waiting for him to visit his stash. We had to make him get up and go. If he saw you produce those coupons, just when your script called for you to be talking about evidence, and if he saw how startled and confused the sight of them made you, he'd be startled and confused himself. And he'd want to make pretty damn sure pretty damn quick that his counterfeits were where he'd left them."

"You could've told me all that. I could've put it across."

"Scotty, if you were that good an actor, you'd still be at Paramount."

I lit my Lucky, finally. "The next thing you'll tell me is that Dunne isn't really dead."

"He'd better be," Paddy said. "I was one of his pallbearers in 1949."

"What about the real IRS?"

"Thanks for reminding me." Paddy keyed his intercom. "Peg,

take a letter to Theodore Mariutto. His address is in our files. 'Dear Mr. Mariutto comma in reference to case number whatever-we-used-in-our-last-letter comma please consider the matter closed period. We regret any inconvenience period. Very truly yours comma.' Type it on that special stationery, sign it with the name we used the last time, and forward it by airmail to your cousin Nabs in Baltimore to be mailed back to California from a Washington post office. Thanks."

I stubbed out my untasted smoke. "The letter Mariutto got was a fake?"

"It was a fake letter," Paddy said. "It was genuine motivation."

"What about the anonymous call to the IRS? I saw you make that myself."

"More motivation. In that case, for you and De Felice, that pustule."

"Paddy, who did you really call?"

"Whom did I call, you mean. Let's not let our standards slip. It was that Chinese restaurant Peggy likes on Santa Monica Boulevard."

The great man leaned back in his seat, scratched at his head until his gray hair was standing up, and then smoothed it carefully. "I don't know what they made of it," he said, "but I'm guessing they'll file their tax returns on time from here on out."

The little pile of wood we'd set burning on the sand popped, sending a stream of sparks up into the night sky. Gabrielle stirred in her chair.

"To sum up," she said, "Rosa Mariutto was rescued, Hollywood Security was six grand and change richer, Moose Mariutto's blackmail files were done to a crisp, and he was none the wiser."

"We were seven grand and change richer," I said. "Paddy sent Moose a bill for our referral fee."

The fire popped again. "You and Paddy were quite the fire bugs. Didn't you also burn down a house near Palmdale?"

"It was a barn near Lancaster."

"Oh, that's okay then." She stretched contentedly. "I knew it would be a good story. That con might have been Paddy's masterpiece. He fooled Moose and you and Guy De Felice and barely left his chair. He was wrong about one thing, though."

"What was that?"

"You are a good actor, Dad. I still remember how you used to dig in to my special pancakes and fried baloney breakfasts."

"Thanks," I said.

"I may make us some tomorrow morning."

"Thanks a lot."

CHAPTER TWENTY

I reported to Hollywood Security the next morning just to see if Hodson McLean had sublet my office. Sadly, he hadn't, but the firm he managed had come through for me in another way. On my desk was a single sheet of paper headed with Helen Gallimore's name, phone number, and current address. Beneath that was a short list of her past addresses and a slightly longer one of jobs she'd held, starting with the one at Ted Mariutto Productions. Only one other item from the job list caught my eye: a brief dip Gallimore had taken in the Los Angeles Police Department's secretarial pool.

The report was uncredited, but I thought I recognized the crisp type of Vickie's IBM Selectric. When I stopped by her desk to thank her, she apologized for submitting a report so short it could fit on a single sheet.

"There wasn't much to dig up. There's no record of Gallimore even being in Los Angeles before 1951. Since then, she doesn't seem to have done anything but work. No marriages, no children, no record that she ever even voted."

Vickie sounded a little wistful, and I remembered that she was unmarried herself.

I must have been looking sympathetic, because she said, "Relax. I vote on a regular basis."

I decided to call Gallimore at her current place of business, a theatrical agency. As I dialed its number, I still hadn't decided whether I'd use Ted Mariutto's name or Amos Decker's to win an interview. It turned out, the only name I needed to mention was my own. Gallimore agreed to see me so quickly it made me think she'd been waiting for my call. She specified a noon meeting at her apartment.

That gave me a couple of hours to kill. I killed them getting verbal updates on our current caseload from operatives right out of college. I gave them the benefit of my wisdom, and they gave me the benefit of their collective doubt. The process made me wonder how many times I'd sat across a desk from Paddy and doubted his wisdom, if not his sanity. He was having the last laugh now, as usual.

A little before noon, I drove to East Hollywood, to a quiet street off Vermont Avenue. It was home to a small courtyard apartment complex whose units had stucco walls and tile roofs and olive trees for shade. Helen Gallimore's courtyard was protected from the sidewalk traffic by a wrought iron gate. Beyond it were some pots that needed watering and a half flight of tiled steps that needed re-grouting. At the top of those steps, in an open doorway, a woman was watching me the way a cat watches the milkman.

If I'd bumped into the Helen Gallimore of 1952 magically transported to 1974, I think I would have recognized her, our only meeting had been that dramatic. But I didn't recognize this woman. She suffered from a common complaint in Southern California: long-term exposure to the sun. But she was suffering from something else, too, something that had dried her from the inside. Her still black hair had escaped the transformation, or so I thought. When I reached the top step, I saw that it wasn't really her hair. It was a wig, long and straight enough to have been sold off by a hippie hard up for pot money. Its youthfulness, in combination with the gaunt face, made the forty-something Gallimore look sixty-something. The wig made me feel sixty-something, every day of it.

"I would never have known you," she said. "Don't tell me you're boxing at your age."

She was looking at the swollen ear I'd collected from one of Bimbo's near misses.

"Not voluntarily," I said.

I handed her a business card, which she studied as she led me inside. Her living room was furnished in dark, heavy pieces that matched the apartment's Mediterranean exterior and somehow suited its occupant as well. She didn't sit down. I wasn't feeling like it either.

"You didn't say on the phone why you wanted to see me, Mr. Elliott."

It was a little late to play coy, since she'd agreed to see me so readily, but I went along.

"I didn't know then myself." I hadn't seen her black wig then, the wig that made me feel my age and more, the wig a witness had mentioned to me in connection with another matter entirely.

"I beg your pardon?"

"I thought I wanted to ask you about your business with Amos Decker. That can wait. First tell me why you went to see Paddy Maguire at the Motion Picture Country House."

Gallimore put the request on hold. "Did Amos Decker tell you we'd done business?"

"No. He kept your secret."

"You say that like it's a virtue, keeping secrets. The people in this town are way too good at that."

"Back to Paddy."

"He was recommended to me years ago by a mutual friend, who happens to be dead. I thought Mr. Maguire might help me learn a secret. I've been trying to learn it for thirty years."

"Did he help?"

"He learned it himself. That's what got him killed. But he never shared it with me."

"What was this secret?"

"I want to know who killed my sister Linda, Mr. Elliott. Do you know?"

"I've never even heard the name Linda Gallimore, not that I recall."

"How about her stage name, Sugar Stapert? Yes, I can see you've heard that name. Mr. Maguire knew it, too. Glass of wine?"

She had two very full glasses poured and waiting for us on a coffee table beside a sofa whose leather was the same dark red as the wine. Gallimore sat down across from one of the glasses, which she immediately seized. I sat beside her, feeling like I actually had taken up boxing again and was back in my corner between rounds, seeing stars.

"Who was this mutual friend who sent you Paddy's way?"

Gallimore was studying my business card, holding it at arm's length to read it. "What happened to your first name?"

"Come again?"

"Thomas. The man who told me about Paddy Maguire and his faithful lapdog always referred to you as Thomas."

"Guy De Felice?"

"Guy De Felice."

She didn't say the name with derision, the way most people did. If anything, her tone was sentimental.

"That's how you know about the con," I said.

"That's how I know *all* about it."

"How did you find your way to De Felice?"

"I didn't. He found his way to me. In 1957. He had something he wanted to sell me, a document my ex-boss Ted Mariutto had stashed away in 1944 that was of special interest to me. According to Guy, Ted had a secret blackmail archive on the people he knew and worked with. I'd heard that myself, but I'd never seen it, not in the five years I worked for Ted. I'd started to think it was just a story."

"By 1957, it was just a story," I said. "Mariutto's archive went up in smoke in 1952."

"That's what you think," Gallimore said. She picked up a bottle that had been hiding next to the sofa and topped off her wineglass, barely stopping at the brim. "The item Guy brought me was the sworn statement of a cleaning woman, Agnes Brown. Agnes found my sister's body. Ted got Brown's story on paper, had it notarized, and then kept it and her away from the police."

"De Felice was conning you," I said. "No papers like that survived."

"You should talk about conning. You and your boss thought you were so smart with that scam you ran on Ted. You never dreamt somebody could be smarter than you or better at your dirty job than you were.

"Guy told me all about the time he worked with Hollywood Security, once we became better acquainted. He even told me parts you didn't know yourself, like how he followed you and Al Alsip after you'd stopped by Guy's office to pay him off. You shook off Alsip in Beverly Hills, but not Guy. He followed you all the way out to San Pedro, and you never saw him once. He slipped inside the Sea Hawk while you were still rooting around in there. After you'd set fire to the place, he saved as much of Mariutto's blackmail files as he could carry. It was a second income for him for years and years.

"You still don't believe me, do you? Funny, Mr. Maguire believed me right away. He knew Guy had outsmarted him."

"Paddy never—" I began and stopped.

I'd remembered something that happened in 1962 on the day Guy De Felice died. The little operative had gotten mixed up with a man more dangerous than Ted Mariutto or even Morrie Bender. Paddy and I had searched De Felice's office when we'd found him missing, looking for a clue in the case we were working, which we found. But we'd found something else as well. Paddy had. A cache of papers. "It seems Guy may have gone in for blackmail in a small way" was all Paddy would say on the subject. Except to add that the papers, which he'd kept, might be embarrassing to "friends of mine."

I was sure now that Paddy had recognized survivors from the Ted Mariutto archive and that Helen Gallimore was telling me the truth.

"How did De Felice find out that you were Stapert's sister?"

"He didn't, not till I told him. He looked me up to put the squeeze on me. Isn't that how you tough guys say it?"

Gallimore got up and crossed to a secretary whose front was carved like the doors of a Gothic cathedral. She pulled out a single sheet of paper, much folded, handed it to me, and drank off her latest glass.

"In that statement, Agnes Brown tells about seeing a woman at the club the night she found the body. Guy thought I might be the woman, since I was in Ted's circle. I was a dark horse who didn't come in for him."

"If that's so," I said, "how do you happen to have the deposition?"

"Not the original, just a copy. I paid more for that than I could afford."

"Looking for a clue to your sister's killer."

"Yes."

"That's why you came to Los Angeles in the first place. You went to work for Mariutto because you knew your sister had been involved with him at the time of her death. How? Did she write you about him?"

"Yes. He was her ticket to the big time, she thought."

"Mariutto didn't know whose sister you were?"

"No. Linda was fair and I was dark. And he didn't know the name Gallimore. Linda had changed hers before she met him."

"How did you manage to land a job with your number one suspect?"

"I was fresh out of business school and young. Ted had an eye for young. And my timing was perfect. He was just back from Omaha and trying to set up as a legitimate producer."

"You were hoping you'd hear something or find something in Mariutto's files about your sister."

"Yes. But I didn't learn much I didn't already know. I already knew that Ted had gone around with my sister for a few months. I found out that he'd two-timed Linda, which I hadn't known but would've guessed, once I'd gotten to know Ted better. He cheated on every woman he was ever with. But I never found out the other woman's name. Ted had gotten rid of his old gang. The only one he'd held onto was Al Alsip, but he could barely talk. Around me, Alsip didn't talk at all.

"The local newspapers weren't much better. Somebody had gotten to them, too. They reported that a woman who sang at the Sea Hawk had been found there shot to death after hours. Then almost nothing."

It didn't take a massive conspiracy to explain why the LA papers had lost track of Stapert. 1944 had been a year of almost continuous battles and casualty lists to match.

"So after a while you decided to look elsewhere. You took a job with the Los Angeles police department."

"Leaving Ted Mariutto Productions wasn't my idea. He fired me. You can only turn a guy like Ted down for sex so many times. I thought the police department was the next best place to look for answers. But their file on the murder was worthless. They never looked for the other woman, never even mentioned her. I understood why when Guy brought me that deposition. Ted had kept Agnes Brown and her statement on ice so he'd have some leverage over the woman who murdered my sister."

"So you bought the deposition from De Felice."

"Not the original. A copy, like I said. Guy thought the original could still be valuable someday. He was sure the deposition wouldn't get me anywhere, and he was right. I could never trace Agnes Brown. She wasn't living in San Pedro anymore, not under that name. I took a copy of the statement to a policeman I'd gotten to know, Captain Wallace, hoping he could find Agnes. What I didn't know was that Wallace moonlighted for Morrie Bender.

"That very night, I was visited by two of Bender's hired thugs. They told me if I ever mentioned Sugar Stapert's name again, they'd cut my throat."

CHAPTER TWENTY-ONE

We sat for a while thinking about that ancient threat. Gallimore actually put a hand to her throat. She caught herself at it and smiled a small, lopsided smile.

I put that smile down to the wine. She'd finished the bottle. Now she looked at my untouched glass.

"Forget it," I said. "I need you awake."

"It's not the wine making me sleepy. It's my medications."

"What medications?"

"You know," she said, "the only thing I really got from the deposition was a little peace of mind about Ted Mariutto. I'd gotten to like Ted, working for him. He was a two-timing heel, but he was a charmer, too."

It was an odd thing for an avenging angel to say. Then again, a woman who could feel sentimental over Guy De Felice could feel sentimental over anybody.

"I never could really believe he was a killer. I'm glad the deposition proved he wasn't."

"All it proves is that a mystery woman ran out of the Sea Hawk that night."

"But Ted would never have kept it from the police if he'd been guilty. He'd have wanted them chasing after the mystery woman."

I thought it more likely, since the police weren't looking for Stapert's killer very hard, that Mariutto had seen the deposition as his hole card, to be played if and only if an honest policeman came his way. I didn't raise that objection, though, because I'd thought of a more damning one.

"If Mariutto wasn't involved in your sister's killing, why did Morrie Bender's men come after you when you started showing that deposition around?"

"I never said he wasn't involved. If a jealous woman killed Linda over him, he was involved. Mr. Bender might have done what he did to keep Ted's name from being dragged through the papers, just when he was making it as a producer."

It seemed like a poor excuse for cutting a woman's throat, but it wasn't out of keeping with what I remembered of Bender.

Someone in the next apartment had decided to listen to music, "A Taste of Honey" by Herb Alpert and the Tijuana Brass.

"Okay," I said. "Morrie Bender's men threatened you in 1957. What happened next?"

"Nothing happened. I was too scared to do anything else."

"How did you get the deposition back from Wallace?"

"I didn't. I'd made copies. But I was afraid to even look at them for a long time."

"Why did you stay in Los Angeles? Why didn't you go home, wherever that is?"

"It was Jackson, Mississippi. It isn't anywhere now. I've asked myself a hundred times why I didn't drop Linda's murder and get away from here. I just couldn't somehow. At first for her sake and then for mine. I'd spent years of my life on it by the time Bender's men came after me. Now it's decades. If I give up, I've wasted my life."

She'd wasted it anyway, I thought. She told me she thought so too by changing the subject.

"When Guy was murdered, I believed it was over the deposition, even though the papers said his murder was tied up with the death of that starlet, Beverly Brooks."

"It was," I said.

"It scared me deeper into my hole anyway. I didn't think about coming out again until Morrie Bender finally died. Ted was dead within a year himself—he drove drunk into a canyon—so it seemed like I'd lost all my chances. I approached some private detectives, but I couldn't afford what they were asking.

"Finally, I thought of Paddy Maguire. I thought if I could hurt his pride by telling him how Guy had outsmarted him, he might look into my sister's murder for nothing. Just to salve his ego."

"How did you find Paddy?"

"Through Hollywood Security. I called them and asked for Mr. Maguire. The girl who answered the phone said he'd retired. I made up some story about being in town briefly and wanting to thank him for an old case he'd handled. She told me where I could find him."

I'd been avoiding the office for weeks, looking for some lead in Paddy's murder, and it had been in our own phone logs all the time.

"I almost didn't go to see him, when I heard he was in an old folks home. When I did go, when I saw how thin and frail he was, I was sure I'd wasted my time. But Mr. Maguire came to life the minute he heard my story and saw the deposition. When I told him that Guy had outsmarted him, he believed me right away, like I said. He knew Guy better than you did.

"When I finished my story, he questioned me like you've been doing. At the end of that, he told me that he'd see to everything. I knew then that I hadn't had to taunt him about Guy to get him to help me. I only had to show him that piece of paper Guy saved from the fire."

I couldn't follow her math, but I wasn't sure enough about anything just then to argue. I said, "So you went home to wait."

"Yes."

"And after a few days, you read in the paper that Paddy was dead."

"Yes."

"Why didn't you go to the police with your deposition then? You would have finally gotten some service. Morrie Bender's dead. Captain Wallace is dead himself or off fishing somewhere. The cops would actually have looked into the Stapert murder, if they'd had proof it had led to Paddy's."

"Are you crazy? When the mob threatened me in '57, I hid for years. And this was worse than any threat. I knew the murderer was still alive and still killing."

She grabbed my wineglass before I could stop her. Her first sip seemed to hit her like a whole bottle. She was suddenly swaying in her seat to the neighbor's music.

"You could have come to me," I said. "De Felice gave you my name. You had Hollywood Security's number."

"I did come to you, Mr. Elliott," she murmured.

"Through Amos Decker."

"Yes. I was too frightened to call you directly. But I knew my time was running out. My last best chance was slipping away."

So was my last best chance. Gallimore's head was starting to droop. But she kept on testifying.

"I read in one of the trade papers that Amos Decker was boasting about topping *The Sting*. I called him right away, pretending to represent a client who had a script about an old con game. When I had him good and interested, I set up a meeting.

"He's a funny man, a funny, little man. So young but so full of himself.

"I admitted to him right away, right away, that there was no script, just a germ of one. A germ. Something that infects you. It didn't bother him. He loved the idea of conmen getting conned themselves. And that there was a murder at the heart of everything. I'd given him exactly the story he wanted."

"You didn't give it to him. You sold it to him for five thousand dollars."

"The money meant a lot to me. I thought. It didn't mean anything to him. He could afford it. He could afford to hire Hollywood Security. I told him he'd have to question you if he wanted to know the details. I knew he'd tell you about Sugar Stapert and the deposition and you would take up where Paddy left off. I was hiring you for free."

That explained the winks and smiles I'd gotten from Decker when I'd told him how well the con had gone.

"It all worked," Gallimore said. "Except that you found your way to me. Are you sure Mr. Decker didn't tell you about me?"

"He's never even gotten around to telling me about your sister. He's been too busy undermining his career. And you didn't need to go through him to hire me. You only needed to tell me that the deposition got Paddy killed. Hollywood Security would have thrown every man on it and never charged you a dime."

"Throw every man on it now, Mr. Elliott. And hurry."

Her eyes were half closed. What I could still see of them was lifeless.

"Just a couple of weeks ago, you were afraid to approach me directly. But when I called you today, you agreed to see me. Something's changed. What?"

She swayed and didn't answer me.

"When you said your time is running out, it wasn't because the witnesses in your sister's case are dying off."

"No." She smiled her lopsided smile again. "I am."

"What is it?"

"Cancer. Breast cancer from five years ago that's spread. I thought Mr. Decker's money would give me more options. More time. I just found out there aren't any more options for me.

"I want to know who killed my sister before I die, Mr. Elliott. I want to know why she died."

She was settling backward as she said it. I took the wineglass from her before it spilled.

"I'll rest now," she said.

CHAPTER TWENTY-TWO

I couldn't rouse Gallimore. After I'd satisfied myself that her breathing had settled into a dependable rhythm, I searched her apartment. I came across three more faded copies of Agnes Brown's deposition and a bathroom full of pills.

In Gallimore's bedroom, I found a spare key for the apartment's front door, which I pocketed. Atop the dresser was a little grouping of family photos, all taken by the same studio. A middle-aged couple, the man dark and serious, the woman blond and smiling, occupied the center frame. They were flanked by their teenage daughters, if what I'd been told was true. The future Sugar Stapert was a knockout, even in black and white, even with the peekaboo bangs that might once have scandalized Jackson but now looked as dated as garters. The young Helen Gallimore seemed much friendlier than the woman I'd met in Ted Mariutto's waiting room, her smile as uncomplicated as the life she'd turned her back on when her sister died.

I locked Gallimore in and returned to my car. My first thought was to drive to Hollywood Security, to report a little progress at last. But I was afraid Hodson McLean would turn the deposition over to the police. So I just sat there behind the Continental's wheel with its ignition key in my hand.

Gallimore's story had taken my feet from under me, as Rosa Wardell's had done a few days earlier. In Wardell's case, the tripwire had been the idea that Paddy had gone to her to volunteer his help.

In Gallimore's, it was Paddy and the deposition. Not the part about Paddy recognizing it. I thought I could explain that away. The original must have been in the papers Paddy had taken from De Felice's office in 1962. Paddy must have read it at his leisure and then remembered it when Helen Gallimore had come calling. What I couldn't explain was why Paddy had gotten out of his rocking chair and gone off to get killed over that deposition. Who or what had he been after?

That question got me back to where everything started and ended, to the blank brick wall that cut me off from Paddy's last case. More than ever, I felt that Paddy had built the wall specifically to block me. Maybe to keep me from stopping a bullet of my own. Maybe to protect me from something else.

It occurred to me that the two unanswered questions about Paddy I'd been handed, Gallimore's and Wardell's, might answer one another, if I could fit them together right. Gallimore was unavailable for questioning at that moment, so I decided to postpone my report to McLean and drive to Thousand Oaks.

According to Wardell, Paddy had offered to help her because he'd had an old score to settle with Ted Mariutto. His reaction to the Agnes Brown statement made sense if the old score involved Sugar Stapert. But I clearly remembered trying to interest Paddy in Stapert back in 1952, after Grove had all but accused Hollywood Security of hushing up her murder. And again later, after Mariutto had led us to the Sea Hawk. My boss had refused to be baited both times.

Of course, Paddy might have been working the Stapert murder without telling me. But then why had he left the deposition behind in Mariutto's secret closet? If the old con had really been conceived to make Mariutto lead us to where evidence in the murder case was stashed—as Helen Gallimore and Amos Decker seemed to believe—why hadn't Paddy searched until he'd found it? Why had he stopped after locating the information about Rosa's father?

The only answer I could think of was that Paddy had never had an old score to settle with Mariutto, not over a murder or anything else. And Paddy hadn't made the initial approach to Rosa. She'd lied about everything, for reasons she'd share with me if I asked her politely.

This time I didn't call ahead. I just showed up at Wardell's rambling manse. There I found a team of gardeners trimming away and no Rosa. Luckily she'd left a forwarding address with one of the hedge trimmer's: the Brookshire Country Club.

I remembered the name from the loving cups and trophies I'd admired in Rosa's study. I hadn't noticed an address amongst all that engraving, so I asked the helpful gardener. He pointed a gloved finger deeper into Wardell's neighborhood. I followed a succession of curving, tree-lined streets until I came to the club's gated entrance.

That gate was open and guarded only by two specimen oak trees, so I drove right in. I looked for Wardell on the tennis courts and then in the Olympic-sized pool before going inside. I checked the dining room and the bar—still without being asked my business by anyone—and then went into the pro shop. I told the pro I had an appointment to sell Wardell insurance and asked if she was still out on the course. He consulted a wall clock as big as the one in Union Station and told me her foursome would be coming up eighteen any moment now.

The pro directed me to a veranda that overlooked the eighteenth green. There I sat in the shade and nursed a beer brought to me by a waitress who looked too young to drink one herself. To pass the time, I read Agnes Brown's deposition. I should say I reread it. I'd scanned it back at Gallimore's while she'd talked herself to sleep.

The single typed sheet was headed "Statement of Agnes Brown." Beneath that was Brown's personal information, such as it was. "Age: thirty-four, Sex: female, Race: colored, Profession: cleaning woman." There was also the address in San Pedro that wasn't any good anymore. The one-paragraph statement followed.

"Early on the morning of November 4, 1944, I arrived at the Sea Hawk Club. Before I could enter the building, the front door opened. I expected to see one of the boys who were always mooning around Miss Stapert, the club's singer, who had a room upstairs. Instead, I saw a woman leave the club and run off. I went inside, using the front door, which was standing open. In the main room, I found Miss Stapert, lying on the dance floor. She was dead. In the blood beside her was a woman's glove. A gray, monogrammed glove."

I could see why De Felice had had trouble cashing in on that particular piece of blackmail material. There was no clue to the identity of the woman who'd rushed from the club. Not even a description of her. Not even what the monogram on her glove had been. Except for that omission, there was more information about the glove than the woman who'd dropped it. That thought set off a flashbulb inside my head. I realized that the one and only purpose of the deposition was to place that glove at the murder scene. So the gray glove had been Mariutto's real leverage over this mystery woman. All of which had been too bad for De Felice, because he hadn't saved the glove from the Sea Hawk fire. He'd overlooked it in his haste.

Or else someone else had gotten to it first. Maybe it hadn't been there for De Felice to find because Paddy had carried it away with him. Maybe the glove had been his real prize all the time, and he'd found it, while I'd been out in the kitchen scaring the mice.

Right then, a second flashbulb fired. I saw why Rosa Wardell would have told me a fairy story about Paddy offering to help her over some old grudge. It was to keep me from figuring out that her husband's real hold on her hadn't been her father's shady business deals. It had been a murder.

Just then, someone stepped between me and the afternoon sun. It was Rosa Wardell. She was in pink today, a pink polo and pink shorts, with a pink sweater draped across her shoulders, its arms crossed on her chest.

"Scotty, I thought it was you. Did you see me hole that chip or were you lost in thought?"

"Not as lost as I had been," I said.

The underage waitress shimmered up. Rosa ordered two of our special drink—the Tom Collins—and banished my beer to the nearest drain. She sat down, not across from me but next to me, the better to knock knees.

"Do you have some news?" she asked.

"Big news," I said. "The con we ran against Mariutto wasn't about recovering blackmail information involving your dear old dad. There probably was never any to begin with. The envelope Paddy showed me, containing the papers I later burned, was probably a dummy he'd ordered up himself.

"The big treasure of that treasure hunt was a bloody glove, evidence in a murder case. It tied a certain woman to the shooting death of a singer named Sugar Stapert. Mariutto had held on to it in case it ever became valuable. Considering he ended up marrying the woman the glove belonged to, that showed real foresight. Oh yeah, the glove was monogrammed. I'm guessing it was RY, for Rosa Yowell."

Wardell was settling in her chair just as Gallimore had done, only without the benefit of drugs. Up until that moment, anyway. Our drinks arrived and Wardell threw down half of hers. Then she said, "Scotty," and choked up.

I took the floor again. "Unfortunately for Paddy, he missed the deposition that tied the glove to the murder scene. It's been floating around Los Angeles for the last twenty-two years, courtesy of your old helpmate, Guy De Felice. De Felice must never have connected the deposition to you, or he wouldn't have lived long enough to get killed over something else. Eventually, it found its way to Paddy. A few days later, Paddy was shot to death, the same as Stapert.

"That part has me foxed. Why would you care about Paddy having that deposition? Care enough to kill him, I mean? You trusted him in 1952. Was it because the statement contradicted the story you'd told him back then, maybe about how Mariutto had framed you for the Stapert killing? Did Paddy finally realize he'd helped the real murderer get off?"

"Whoa, Scotty, please. You're scaring me. You can't think I'd hurt Mr. Maguire. He saved me."

"I remember. Showed up out of the blue and offered to help you."

"It's true. And he did help me. Those papers on Daddy weren't phonies. They were the real thing. I remembered enough about them from seeing them in Paddy's office to ask Daddy about them later. He owned up to everything.

"Look, I told you Paddy had his own agenda. I told you that I never knew what it was. So it was over a glove. It wasn't my glove. I was a sophomore in high school back in Omaha in 1944. I can show you my yearbook. I hadn't even met Ted then, never mind Sugar Stapert."

"Then how do you happen to know the year she was killed?"

"I was married to Ted; of course I heard about her murder. But I learned something pretty damn quick, and that was never to ask Ted about her. Some of his mob buddies still had wives from the old days, and they told me a little.

"Stapert was a mantrap. All the men had a thing for her, even Al Alsip, that little cornhusk. The trouble was, she liked most of the men back. Ted got tired of that after a while—no two-timer can stand being two-timed—and he threw her over for somebody else. Don't ask me who; I don't know. Whoever it was never got introduced to the old wives club. Sugar knew, though, and threatened to cause trouble. Not long after that, she was dead."

CHAPTER TWENTY-THREE

This time I did drive to Hollywood Security. Hodson McLean was out, which saved me a moral dilemma over the deposition. The faithful Vickie was still at her post, and she had a message for me. Captain Grove of the LAPD had called to give me a belated progress report. I was to call him back.

I had a hand on the phone when a better idea came to me. I told Vickie to call the captain and ask him to meet me at the Intersection Lounge. Then I wrote down Agnes Brown's vital statistics and her old San Pedro address and asked Vickie to trace her, using all the operatives we had if she saw fit. All but one. I asked her to have that one collect newspaper articles on the Sugar Stapert murder. Gallimore had pronounced them worthless, but I wanted to judge for myself.

The Intersection Lounge was in Hollywood proper. At the epicenter of Hollywood, in fact, at the legendary crossroads of Hollywood and Vine. I'd broken a case there once, a very sad case, though I didn't hold that against the Intersection. Not when the guy who worked behind its L-shaped bar mixed a Gibson that was second only to my own. Unfortunately, the lounge also had a pianist whose playing always reminded me of the old biblical injunction: "Never let your left hand know what your right hand is doing." Luckily, the lady was off somewhere, maybe having her ear tuned, so I was able to sip my drink in peace.

At least, I could have if I'd never gone to see Helen Gallimore.

Since then, I hadn't had a peaceful moment. Rosa Wardell had convinced me that she had no prior knowledge of a bloody glove. But I was more certain than ever that Paddy had had such knowledge and that the whole con had been cooked up to separate Mariutto from that glove.

That left me with another question to answer. If Paddy really had drafted Rosa Mariutto, which appeared to be true after all, why had he done it? He could have worked the whole business without involving her and still recovered the glove. He might have known about Rosa's situation and decided to kill two birds with one stone. But a more likely explanation was that he'd used Rosa to protect the identity of his real client, the lady of the gray glove. Protect it from everyone, me included. Maybe me especially.

I was seated at one corner the bar's ninety degree angle, the corner that commanded a view of the front door. I saw Captain Grove enter, looking as rumpled and tired as I felt. He sat down on the other side of the angle, took off his hat, displaying his thinning but well oiled hair, and ordered a rye and water. Then he opened with a sneer, as he usually did.

"You'll be the last guy in America drinking those damned Gibsons. You'll have to carry around your own bottle of onions."

"It's close to that right now," I said.

"What's the idea of having your secretary call me back? When I call, I expect a call back from you, not from a flunky with a counteroffer."

"I thought you probably could use a drink," I said.

"Uh huh. Now let's have your real reason. With Hollywood Security, I know the first answer is always a lie."

Paddy had favored that approach. He'd also taught me to have the second lie ready to go.

"You said you were calling with a progress report on Paddy's murder. I was afraid the report would be no progress and you'd tell me you were giving up. I didn't think I could talk you out of it over the phone."

"You couldn't talk me out of it with a violin accompaniment. Look, Elliott, there just isn't anything for us to go on. The old fixer covered his tracks too well. It hurts me to say it, but if you've come up with any leads, I'll take them."

"You told me not to look into Paddy's murder."

"And I told myself I was wasting my breath when I said it. What have you got?"

I had an old deposition that had reproduced like a young rabbit. I left it in my pocket. Before I'd driven to Thousand Oaks, my pride had kept me from turning it over to the police. Now I had a better reason.

"Nothing," I said. "The agency's loaned me out to a kid director."

"Name of Amos Decker? Don't look so surprised. Your name popped up in a police report on a fracas at Decker's beach house. He catch you with your hand in the silver drawer?"

"Something like that," I said, relieved to have the subject changed, even at the expense of my reputation. I could have changed it just by reaching for my glass, if I'd only known. I reached for it now, and my coat sleeve drew back, revealing Billy's MIA bracelet.

"You're wearing that now?" Grove asked.

"I'm wearing it now."

"I'd never of guessed you'd fall for that mumbo jumbo."

"What you mean, 'mumbo jumbo'?"

Grove tasted his neglected drink. "I mean, you can't really believe a copper band can keep somebody alive. Isn't that how those bracelets work? As long as somebody with a heartbeat is wearing that thing, your son isn't really dead?"

"No," I said. "As long as somebody's wearing this thing, my son isn't forgotten."

"Don't kid yourself. Every guy we sent to that side of the world was forgotten the minute the anchor on his transport was raised. That was true in our war, and it was true in your kid's."

"His name was Billy," I said.

"Was is right," Grove said, but he raised his glass to him. I did, too.

"You met him once," I said. "When you came to our house to compare notes on another murder."

I'd been playing with Billy on the living room floor and Ella had been fixing dinner. That little taste of domesticity had frightened Grove like no gun could. He hadn't been able to get away fast enough.

"Nothing wrong with my memory," he said.

"Good. I want to ask you about something. Something that may have to do with Billy, in a way."

I hadn't thought to use that gambit until Grove spotted Billy's bracelet. I was a little ashamed to use it, though I knew Billy wouldn't have minded. Not in the service of this particular cause.

"I knew we'd get around to the real business of the meeting sooner or later," Grove said.

"I want to know how you got off Paddy's payroll, way back when."

"You asking for trouble, Elliott?"

"No, just an answer. When I joined Hollywood Security, Paddy had a paid source on the LAPD. Turned out to be you. Paddy had a saying about paid informants. 'Pay once, own forever.' He meant that once an informant had taken a bribe, the threat of exposing him would keep him in line.

"But it didn't work with you. Only a year or so after I met you, you were off the payroll for good and no harm done to your career. I've always wondered about that. Now I'm asking how you did it."

"What's that got to do with your kid?"

"I'll tell you in a minute."

Grove drained his glass. "Forget it. I don't owe you any favors."

"Then I'll owe you one."

"You owe me one for every day you've stayed out of jail. But you wouldn't thank me for this one."

"What's that supposed to mean?"

"That you don't want to know the answer."

"So you're doing me a favor by not telling me? I thought you didn't owe me any."

Grove gave me the BB eyes for as long as it took him to check my math. Then he addressed the man behind the bar, who'd been doing his best to blend into the wallpaper. "Another round on his tab and then get lost."

When the bartender had fired and fallen back, Grove said, "It was you, Elliott. You got me off the old mick's hook."

"How?"

"By getting engaged to a Warners publicist named Pidgen Englehart," he said, using two of Ella's old names, her studio nickname and her maiden name. "You two got married in '48, right? That was when I was finally able to kiss Maguire good-bye, so to speak. I'd heard something about your fiancée that Maguire didn't want you to hear. I used it to buy my way out. I'm not proud of it, but there it is."

"What did you hear?"

"I say again, you don't want to know."

"If it was how wild Ella was during the war, she told me that herself. It was over her brother getting killed in action. It didn't mean anything."

"Maguire paid up for nothing, then."

Grove suddenly wasn't making eye contact.

"It was more than that," I said. "What was it?"

The policeman shrugged. "I happened to hear that she'd had a little fling with a junior member of the local mob, a man I've always believed to be an unpunished murderer. He ended up driving himself drunk into a canyon, so I guess he got punished in the end. It was Moose Mariutto."

I reached for my glass but found I couldn't lift it, even though Grove had given me the answer I'd been expecting, the answer that made everything else add up.

Grove was having no trouble with his own glass. "Now tell me why you wanted to know that so badly." He nodded toward the MIA bracelet. "And what it has to do with him."

Paddy's training saved me then. I'd worked out my last ditch answer in advance, as he'd taught me to.

"Ella and I have been separated for over a year. I've been trying to make up my mind one way or the other, to stay in limbo or file for a divorce. I've always suspected that you used Ella to break free. I wanted to know for sure. And I wanted to know what it was all about. I thought it might tip the scales for me."

"What does that have to do with your boy?"

I hadn't worked that part out in advance, but I didn't miss a beat. "That's what broke us up to begin with, Billy going missing and Ella not being able to let it go."

Grove got philosophical then for only the second time in our long acquaintance. "Some things you can't let go of. Not without selling out your whole life."

CHAPTER TWENTY-FOUR

After Grove stalked out, I took my time settling my tab. So much time that I came close to ordering my third Gibson, even though that would have put me out of action. Luckily, the Intersection's piano player showed up for her evening shift and scared me out the door.

I drove to East Hollywood in flypaper traffic, though I was again in no particular hurry. I'd been pretty sure when I'd left her that Gallimore had been down for the count. I was desperate for a line on Agnes Brown, though. Gallimore had failed to trace her, but she might have dug up something that could help me now.

In the end, I didn't get any new leads or even another go at Gallimore. When I let myself into her apartment, I found she'd managed to relocate from the living room sofa to her bed. But she'd also found another bottle of wine and was more out of it than when I'd tucked her in.

I poured out the rest of the bottle, rolled her onto her stomach to cut down the chances of her choking on her own vomit, and left. The trip to East Hollywood had been a stall in any case. So, for that matter, was my determination to track down Agnes Brown. The obvious trail led to Ella, and I followed it, finally.

Caverna Drive was showing signs of post-suppertime life. The street had to serve as the neighborhood's collective backyard, as the real yards climbed like junior Alps on one side of Caverna and dropped away like ski slopes on the other. I drove slowly past a man and a boy tossing a baseball back and forth and then braked completely for a line of bicyclists, some wobbling between training wheels, who were following one another down the pavement like a line of baby ducks.

I squeezed the Continental into Ella's tiny driveway and climbed out in time to field a basketball that was rolling down the gutter. Its rightful owner didn't ask me to join him for a game of horse, luckily, or I might have stalled some more. Not that it would have mattered in the end. When I knocked on Ella's door, no one answered.

I retrieved my pipe from the car, leaving my jacket and tie in exchange, and sat down on the concrete step that doubled as Ella's front porch. I would have preferred her cantilevered back porch and its view of the valley, which would shortly be a carpet of lights, but I would have needed mountain climbing equipment to reach it. So I filled my pipe and lit it and made myself as comfortable as I could.

By and by, the neighborhood mothers appeared on their own concrete steps to call their children and husbands in, and I was left alone with my thoughts. I didn't enjoy their company. As so often happened, the answers I'd found had only raised new questions.

For example, I thought I now understood why Paddy had approached Rosa Mariutto in 1952. He'd somehow found out about her divorce troubles and seen those as the perfect screen for an operation against Mariutto, an operation whose real goal hadn't been to free the black marketeer's wife but my own.

But free her from what exactly? Assuming, as I now did, that she was the woman who'd left the gray glove in the Sea Hawk in 1944, what had prompted Mariutto to threaten to use it in 1952?

I wasn't assuming that Ella had killed Sugar Stapert. I wouldn't believe that, not until Ella told me so herself. And maybe not then. But I was sure the threat of being accused of the killing had driven everything that had happened.

Another new question my new answers had raised was this: Why had Paddy given Gallimore such prompt service when she'd brought him the deposition? He couldn't have seen it as a threat to Ella. There wasn't anything in the Brown statement that could hurt her. Not after all these years, not if the glove had been discovered and destroyed in 1952. So Paddy must have seen something in the deposition other than a threat to my wife. Maybe it was a chance to solve one last murder and win one last headline. So why had he gone to such elaborate lengths to cover his tracks? Was it simply to guard Ella's reputation and my feelings? Or was it because what he'd spotted in the deposition was dangerous, not to Ella but to whoever tried to follow his trail?

By the time I reached that point in my thinking, my pipe was wet from overuse and the sun was deep in the Pacific. One of the neighbors was coming out of his front door every fifteen minutes to see if my car was still there—or to let me know that he was still there and alert to my every move. I thought about leaving Ella a note, but in the end I just headed home.

I'd skipped my lunch, if you didn't count cocktail onions. Now I drove past restaurant after restaurant without stopping for a late dinner. When I got home, I put an album on the turntable, Ellington's *Newport 1958*, but I never lowered the tone arm. The crash of the ocean, coming in through the windows I'd opened to cool the house, fit my mood better. I sat down in the dark to listen. And I fell asleep.

The next morning, I woke up with a stiff neck that was as much psychological as physical. I tried walking it out on the beach and then steaming it out in the shower. Neither worked. Nor did toast and coffee, when I finally got around to noticing how hungry I was. I called Ella's and got no answer, which my sore neck liked not at all.

I didn't have a key to Ella's house, but I had one to Helen Gallimore's. So I drove back to East Hollywood for my second interview with Sugar Stapert's sister.

A coffee shop on Gallimore's corner was doing a good Saturday morning business. I picked up two large black coffees and a bag of sweet rolls. Not the normal things a private eye brought to a grilling, but I'd never been a normal private eye. I figured that Gallimore had probably had a worse night's sleep than I'd had and that some caffeine and sugar might get the interview off on the right foot.

There was a woman standing in Gallimore's little forecourt, a pear-shaped woman dressed in a housecoat and slippers. When she saw me, she took a step back toward the open door of the neighboring apartment. Then the sight of my cardboard tray of rolls and coffee seemed to reassure her.

"You here to see Helen?" she asked. "Something's wrong in there. She's not answering my knock. And last night, I heard a sound. I'm not sure. It might have been a car backing into something. But it sounded like it came from Helen's."

I asked her to hold my peace offerings and unlocked Gallimore's front door. The blinds I'd left open in the front room were now closed, keeping out the light and holding in an acrid odor I knew only too well. I followed it into the bedroom. I found Helen Gallimore lying on the bed where I'd left her. She was now on her back. On her face was a pillow, scorched in its center by a gunshot.

When I turned from that sight, I saw something that dropped the temperature of my blood a few degrees. The little grouping of family photos on the dresser had been moved slightly. And the portrait of Linda Gallimore, aka Sugar Stapert, was gone.

I checked the ornately carved secretary in the front room. The copies of the deposition I'd left there were also missing.

CHAPTER TWENTY-FIVE

Over the years, Paddy and I had had more than one spirited discussion on the subject of reporting crimes to the police. With Helen Gallimore's murder, I came close to the Patrick J. Maguire point of view, which he'd once summarized as "what the police don't know won't hurt you." I knew that even half a day's freedom of action might make all the difference to me now. Unfortunately, I had a witness to contend with, the lady of the housecoat, whose name turned out to be Wasserman. Just as I closed the secretary, she arrived at the open front door. She was crying.

"Was it the cancer?" she asked.

"No," I said.

I didn't ask her how she knew Gallimore was dead. Her nose might have been as good as mine or her work experiences as interesting. Or Gallimore's declining health might have had Wasserman keyed up and ready. Her follow-up questions supported that guess.

"Did she have a fall? Is that what I heard last night?"

"No," I said again.

I took the cardboard coffee tray from her and sat her on Gallimore's burgundy sofa. Then I used the living room phone to call Ed Sharpe. I didn't cross my fingers while I dialed but I could have, the chances of actually getting Sharpe were that thin. But get him I did, not only on the phone, which he picked up like we'd had the call scheduled for weeks, but also in person, only a few minutes after the patrol cars he'd dispatched.

"We meet in bad places," he said when he finally had time to devote to me.

I'd always admired Sharpe's ability to rise above the kind of work he'd chosen to do. On that particular morning, though, it seemed to be getting to him. The skin of his face was sagging, and his pencil-line moustache looked like it was going to seed.

"I know who called me in," Sharpe said. "Who called you?"

I'd used my waiting time to work out a story, one that might win me my half day. But I didn't like my chances of telling it the same way twice. "We're not waiting for Captain Grove?"

"You caught a break there. He was called downtown this morning on a street gang killing, a bad one. He'll be reporting to the mayor, once they get it sorted out.

"Tell me why you showed up this morning carrying Danish pastries—thanks for those, by the way—and how you happen to have a key to the victim's apartment."

We started pacing as we talked, first in the little courtyard and then along the street beyond the iron fence.

"Some background first," I said. "Earlier this week, I was sent by Hollywood Security to see Amos Decker the director."

"The Wildman of Malibu, the men in blue call him. Go on."

"Decker had told my boss he was in fear of his life, but he really wanted to rent my memory for a few days. Someone had sold him the outline of a con game Hollywood Security ran in 1952. The mark was Ted Mariutto. Decker wanted me to fill in the gaps. He wants to use the story for a movie script."

Sharpe, who knew what town he lived in, said, "Wants to rip off *The Sting*, does he? I hope this time they get Redford to cut his hair."

"I went along with the project because I wanted to know who had sold Decker the idea."

"Why?"

"For one thing, nobody was supposed to know the whole story except Paddy and me. For another, Paddy was shot not too long ago. I'm down to grasping at straws on that, and the old con popping up again seemed like a likely straw."

"And Decker gave you Gallimore's name?"

"No, he'd taken an oath not to. But he took off for Vegas and I got a chance to go through his checkbook register. I found Gallimore's name in it and eventually I found Gallimore.

"She agreed to an interview yesterday after lunch. As soon as I laid eyes on her, I knew I was onto something. She was wearing a long black wig."

Sharpe actually whistled. "I spotted the hairpiece, even with the blood. I didn't connect it to Maguire, but I should have. When I interviewed the staff at his retirement home, one of his nurses mentioned a lady visitor wearing a long black wig."

"The nurse mentioned it to me, too. Gallimore admitted to being Decker's source. She'd worked as Ted Mariutto's secretary back in the fifties and been half in love with him."

"Old Moose could charm the ladies," Sharpe said.

"Sometime after she left Mariutto, she was approached by Guy De Felice. Did you know him?"

"Well enough to scratch every time I hear his name."

"De Felice was involved in the '52 operation we ran against Mariutto. We recovered some blackmail material Mariutto was holding over the head of our client. We were careless, though, and De Felice walked away with a lot of damaging information on innocent bystanders."

"Not so innocent bystanders," Sharpe corrected. "Who was your client back then?"

Up to that point, I'd been telling Sharpe the straight truth. Now I left the trail, machete in hand.

"Torrance Beaumont." I apologized silently for that, but the free-living Beaumont was a likely candidate for blackmail as well as a dead one. Which also made him a dead end, as far as Sharpe and Grove were concerned.

"Why did De Felice show up on Gallimore's door?"

"Because she'd been Mariutto's secretary. Some of the blackmail victims were only identified by initials. De Felice thought she might be able to decipher a few of those. In exchange, he told her about the old con. To do that, he had to tell her about Paddy. I guess De Felice laid it on thick. Years later, when Gallimore needed a detective, she remembered Paddy and looked him up."

"She needed a detective why?"

"To investigate a mysterious death that might have been a

murder. The death of her ex-employer and love interest, Ted Mariutto."

I'd been improvising and then some, but now I was deep in the weeds. Several people had mentioned Mariutto's death in a one-car accident, though nobody had hinted at murder. But I needed a reason for Gallimore to have approached Paddy that didn't involve Sugar Stapert, and Mariutto seemed like the only substitute.

I was surprised, then, to get a nod of agreement out of Sharpe.

"At the time Moose drove through that guardrail, there were rumors going around the department. Morrie Bender, Mariutto's protector, had gotten his not that long before. Old Moose had thumbed his nose at a lot of well-connected people while hiding behind Bender. The thinking was that one or more of those offended citizens had helped him find that canyon."

"But why would your old boss take up something that was going to lead him straight to the mob? He was smarter than that. Unless he'd just gotten tired of living."

"What if Paddy went after someone who wasn't that well connected? What if it was Al Alsip?"

Alsip's name came readily to hand. He'd been on my mind ever since Rosa Wardell had listed him among Sugar Stapert's conquests.

"Little Al?" Sharpe repeated. "Yeah, I could see Maguire bracing him without much worry, in a dark alley or anywhere else. But Alsip kill Moose? He was Moose's right hand. At least, he was until Moose gave up playing producer. Why would Alsip turn on him?"

"I'd like to ask him."

"Good luck with that. I haven't heard a word about Alsip in a while. Come to think of it, he dropped out of sight around the time Moose let him go. Don't make too much of that. Some people actually do leave LA you know. Not everyone hangs around after their reason for being here dries up and blows away."

"Let's not get personal," I said.

"Okay, Gallimore wanted Paddy to look into Moose's death. Why now? Why after four years?"

"Gallimore had terminal cancer. She wanted to know who had killed her ex-lover before she died herself."

If the con had been Paddy's masterpiece, the story I'd just told

Sharpe was mine, at least in the category of police interrogations. All the pieces fit together, roughly, but I'd managed not to mention Sugar Stapert, Agnes Brown, and Ella, to name only the major omissions.

"Okay," Sharpe said again, "So you left Miss Gallimore how?"

"Passed out," I said. "She was drinking the whole time I was with her. And she was on some medications, I don't know what."

"There's a whole pharmacy in the bathroom."

"I know," I said. "I searched the place yesterday. When you get done fingerprinting, you're going to have enough of my mine to frame me for six murders."

"Captain Grove will settle for one. You always search the homes of new clients? Most PIs just do a credit check."

"She got Paddy killed. She claimed not to know how, but I wasn't taking her word for that."

"And?"

"I didn't find any answers. When I came back here this morning—"

"Wait a damn minute. I'm not finished with yesterday."

Sharpe's tone wasn't friendly, but his warning was. I knew he was telling me that he'd already questioned Mrs. Wasserman. She must have been on surveillance duty yesterday evening as well, when she wasn't busy changing Herb Alpert records on her Victrola.

"I locked Gallimore in around one o'clock. I'd come across a spare key when I'd searched the place. I came back a little after five for another talk, but she'd found a bottle of wine I'd overlooked, so I tucked her in for the night."

That tallied for Sharpe. "The neighbor lady saw you come and go. She didn't see anything after that, unfortunately, but she might have heard a shot a little after ten. So you came back this morning and what?"

"I met Mrs. Wasserman in the courtyard. She said something was wrong in Gallimore's apartment. I left Wasserman outside and went in. You saw what I saw. I didn't touch the body."

"Search the apartment again?"

I took that as another warning about Mrs. Wasserman's eagle eyes. "Not to speak of," I said. "I opened the secretary to see if the pocketbook I'd seen the day before was still there. It was. I had the impression someone else had done some looking around. I can't say why." Not without giving away the family jewels.

Sharpe stopped pacing. "Notice the portrait grouping in the bedroom?" he asked, as close to eager as I'd ever seen him.

"Not this morning," I lied.

"There were three photos in it. Two were black and whites and one was color."

"I don't think there was a color one yesterday."

"The color picture wasn't a portrait at all, not a family portrait. It was the photo of a model you get when you buy a frame. Instead of removing it, some people just stick their own photo in front of it. Gallimore was one of them. The shooter must have taken the black-and-white photo away. Remember anything about it?"

"Not really. I think it was a portrait of a teenage girl."

"It was. According to Wasserman, it was Gallimore's sister."

I was seriously regretting not binding and gagging Wasserman while I'd had the chance. Then Sharpe added, "That's all she's been able to recall so far."

He resumed his pacing, and I fell in beside him.

"I can't see a connection between Moose Mariutto and Gallimore's sister, Scotty. For that matter, I can't figure out what brought the murderer here last night. It's too big a coincidence, assuming it's the same guy who helped Mariutto across in 1970. I mean him waiting four years to find Gallimore and then showing up on the very day you spoke to her. Grove will chew that up and spit it out."

I said, "Something Gallimore told Paddy led him to Mariutto's killer. Paddy was shot not quite three weeks ago. That's how long it took the killer to trace Paddy's trail back to Gallimore."

My made-up version sounded fantastic when I said it out loud, and yet the truth was more fantastic by far. Sugar Stapert's killer had found Gallimore on the same day I did, not after a layoff of four years but thirty.

"It's still a coincidence him finding her yesterday," Sharpe said. "How's this? The murderer has been keeping tabs on you. He knew you'd be looking into Paddy's murder, either because he knew how the old Hollywood Security worked or because you contacted him while you were trying to get a line on Paddy's last investigation. You've probably talked to half the people in Los Angeles in the past three weeks."

"And that someone's been tailing me ever since?" I would have added that I could spot a tail better than that, but somewhere very warm, De Felice would have been laughing his head off.

"Why not? You led him to Gallimore, and he took her out. Only now he doesn't know how much she told you. You've got two bull's-eyes on your back, buddy, the murderer's and Captain Grove's. If I were you, I'd consider an ocean voyage."

"I'll just have to find the killer before he or Grove finds me."

"You've been at that for three weeks. Think you've got another three coming?"

We looked down the block toward Vermont Avenue, expecting to see Grove's unmarked car. I was, anyway.

"No, I don't. Ed, I need a favor."

"Another one? If I let you walk away from here today, I'm jumping on a grenade for you."

"I need to find Al Alsip." I hadn't known I needed to find Alsip, not until I'd mentioned him to Sharpe to fill a hole in the story I'd been improvising. But now I was sure I did.

"I wouldn't mind talking to him myself," Sharpe said. "I'll see what I can do. Now get out of here while you're still able."

CHAPTER TWENTY-SIX

I drove straight to Ella's. After my recent soul-baring with Grove about my marital woes, I didn't expect him to look for me on Caverna Drive. Then again, if he managed to connect Gallimore to Sugar Stapert, Grove might show up there looking for Ella, since I'd cleverly refreshed his memory of her wartime relationship with Mariutto. That was a remote risk, but even if it had been a likely one, I would have gone to Caverna Drive. It was the place I had to go.

Remembering the reception I'd gotten on my last visit, I was prepared to hold Ella's front door open with my foot. That turned out to be unnecessary. Ella opened the door, took one look at me, and fell into my arms.

"Scotty! I was praying you'd come."

I squeezed her back, but not for as long as I wanted to. I was too conscious of the game clock. I guided her into her spartan living room, and we sat on a couch that had almost as much give as the maple floor.

"How did you know?" she asked. "Did one of the neighbors see me?"

As sure as I was in my heart that Ella couldn't have hurt Gallimore or anyone else, her questions froze me. Understandably, perhaps, as I'd just come from a crime scene that featured a nosy neighbor.

Luckily for me, Ella kept talking. "I almost left a note on your door. This is better, though, you showing up out of nowhere just when I needed you. It's like a movie script. It's like our lives used to be."

"You came by the beach house?"

"Yes, last night a little before dusk. When I couldn't raise you, I went out onto the beach and watched the sun go down. I got to thinking about the last time I watched the sun set from that beach, back when we first heard about Billy. I found you and Gabby waiting for me on a dune that night. I was hoping you'd be there again last night, but you weren't."

"No," I said.

"Where were you, Scotty?"

"Here, on your front step. You can ask the guy across the street. He thought I was a really slow burglar."

I was hoping one of my Malibu neighbors had taken as much interest in Ella, hoping it very sincerely.

"Why were you here?" Ella asked.

"Let's finish your story first. Why did you come to see me last night?"

That was just a warm-up for the real question: Why had Ella suddenly needed me last night when she hadn't for so long?

I could hear Ed Sharpe on the subject. He hadn't liked the coincidence of the murderer finding Gallimore on the very day I did. He wouldn't like the coincidence of Ella deciding that she couldn't live without me on the very night Gallimore was shot, if he ever found his way to Caverna Drive. Captain Grove would like it even less.

Then Ella drew me back from the pit a second time. "Gabby came to see me yesterday; I think right after she left you. She told me you'd been in a fight and that she'd heard all about the old Mariutto con. She enacted the whole story, even imitating Paddy's voice and yours, like she used to do as a kid. She was laughing the whole time, and I was dying inside.

"Gabby didn't know—you don't know—that the con was really about me."

"Tell me about it," I said.

Ella sat there for a moment, her gray blue eyes out of focus, the tiny lines around them softening. If she had been any other witness,

I would have been steeling myself for a lie. But I knew Ella, the screenwriter, was simply deciding how best to tell the truth.

"You know about me and the war years," she finally said. "How I carried on after my brother was killed. I think it was one of the first things I told you about myself."

"It was," I said.

"You thought I was being honest with you—I wanted to be—but I held something back. Someone back. Ted Mariutto.

"I met him on the Warner Bros. lot. He was movie crazy even in his black-market days. He took special care of the Warners front office as far as his illegal gasoline and steaks went. I guess he was looking ahead, though I didn't spot it then. I met him one day in the commissary and thought he was fascinating. He looked like a refugee Balkan prince and sounded like a longshoreman. It took me a while to realize that there was more longshoreman there than prince. A lot more.

"It also took me a while to spot that Ted was keeping me under wraps, only taking me to out-of-the-way places and insisting on a lot of quiet evenings at home. Sorry, Scotty."

She'd mistaken a distracted look in my eyes for hurt feelings. I'd actually been silently thanking the dead black marketeer for his discretion. It had saved Ella later, when Agnes Brown's deposition had started making the rounds.

"Go on," I said.

"I finally found out that Ted was practically engaged to a singer named Sugar Stapert. I was warned about her by my boss in the Warners publicity department, Chester Edson. He told me that Stapert was bad news, and he didn't know the half of it. She was wilder than I'd ever been and violent on top of it. I learned that when she showed up at my desk at Warners one day, carrying a little pearl-handled revolver.

"She told me to stop seeing Ted or else. She actually said 'or else,' like a character in a movie. She sounded like a movie, too, like Vivien Leigh playing Scarlet O'Hara drunk. Not that she looked the part. She was a pint-size blonde with pointy little teeth and a casual attitude about buttoning up her clothes.

"I told her to go to hell, but the truth was I'd had enough of Ted. Those days were one long binge for me, but every once in a while I'd have a lucid moment. During one of those, I saw Ted for what he was. I told myself it was one thing to run around with soldiers in wartime and another to be with a man who would have helped the other side win if it had made him a buck.

"But it was also one thing to dump Ted and another to get rid of Sugar Stapert. Even after I'd told Ted good-bye, I kept getting hang-up calls at all hours. Then the front window of my apartment was broken. Then the tires on my car were slashed. I would rather she'd slashed my upholstery. I would have had less trouble getting that replaced.

"Finally, I decided to have it out with her. I drove to the club where she worked and lived, the Sea Hawk. Ted had tried to maroon her out there when she'd gotten too hard for him to handle, but she always managed to get loose. She always had men hanging around her, and they always had cars.

"I went after hours to avoid Ted, but I overdid it. I was too long working up my nerve, I guess. The place was dark when I got there, but not locked up. In fact the front door was standing open.

"Like a fool, I went in. I found Stapert lying on the dance floor. She'd been shot in the chest. I tried to find her pulse, but there wasn't one. I'd taken off my glove to do that and I left it there when I ran out. It was monogrammed, of course. There's no point in leaving something at a murder scene if it isn't monogrammed. Even beginning screenwriters laugh at that cliché. I always shudder."

CHAPTER TWENTY-SEVEN

"*I thought I'd* be arrested, Scotty. I really did. I looked for the police every day."

She got up and walked to a window. A front window, overlooking the street, which she scanned, as though expecting those 1944 police to show up finally. I fought the urge to join her at it.

"Nothing happened," Ella said. "No knock on the door. No calls from policemen or even reporters. Hardly any stories about Sugar Stapert to follow in the papers. I was safe. That brush with disaster made me clean up my life. That and meeting you, Scotty.

"Flash forward to 1952. I'm now married to a wonderful guy. We have a beautiful son. I'm working on my first really good script, *Private Hopes*. And then the knock on the door finally comes. But it isn't a policeman or a reporter. It's Ted Mariutto.

"He'd left town after the war, when some congressional committee finally got around to looking into black marketeering, and I'd hoped I'd never see him again. Then there he was, on the front porch of our old place in Doyle Heights. He was a little grayer at the temples, but just as manicured on the outside and rough on the inside. He told me he was setting himself up as a producer at Warners, my old studio. He'd heard about *Private Hopes*. And he wanted it.

"You remember the crazy agent I had back then."

"Mona," I said.

"Mona. She was telling everybody who'd listen that I had a script that would win some lucky producer the Best Picture Oscar. Ted wanted to be that producer. I told him no."

Ella walked back to where I sat, but didn't join me on the couch. "That's when Ted told me he could prove I'd murdered Sugar Stapert. He said he had my glove, stained with Stapert's blood. He'd give it to the police unless I sold him my script.

"I didn't know what to do, Scotty. I didn't think any jury would convict me on that evidence. I told Ted that. He laughed and agreed with me, but he said I'd have lost everything long before the jury brought in a verdict. You and Billy, he meant. My career. Even *Private Hopes*. He said no producer would look at it after I'd been arrested. No producer would look at me."

I knew the feeling. Throughout her story, Ella had been looking anywhere but at me. Now she did.

"Whoever wrote this scene didn't give you many lines," she said.

"Whoever did must know I work better without them," I said. "Like Mary Pickford."

"Scotty. When's the last time you ate anything?"

"I had breakfast." I didn't add that the toast and coffee had also served as lunch and dinner for the previous day. "When's the last time you ate?" I asked.

"Does watching Gabrielle eat count?"

I stood up and took her by the hand. "Lead me to the kitchen."

I actually didn't need to be led, having taken Gabrielle's verbal guided tour. Plus the house had a floor plan that made minimal use of walls. I'd glimpsed what I took to be the kitchen each time I'd been there. It was tucked behind a partition wall that didn't quite reach the ceiling and was all cabinets on the kitchen side.

I'd already had breakfast, but Ella's larder didn't offer many alternatives. "How about gashouse eggs?" I asked.

"Fine," Ella said.

The better places called them eggs in a basket, but Paddy, who'd introduced me to them, always called them gashouse eggs. They were the only things I'd ever seen him cook, maybe the only things he could cook. Peggy had kept him at fighting weight, until she'd taken to her bed.

I dug out Ella's largest skillet and got some butter melting on her gas range top.

"Just one for me," she said.

"I remember. Grab the orange juice."

I dug out three slices of bread and selected a likely glass from one of her open-shelf units, a glass with a two-inch bore. I used it like a biscuit cutter to remove a circle of bread from the center of each slice. By then the butter was sizzling in the pan. I threw in the three slices and the three bread circles.

"Some people toast the bread first," Ella observed.

"Paddy never did."

"Right, Paddy," Ella said with a nod, as though I'd cited Pope Paul.

"You went to see Paddy after Mariutto came to see you."

I was giving Ella a break by jumping us ahead to Paddy instead of asking why she hadn't come to me. She accepted it quickly.

"Yes," she said. "I told Ted that the script wasn't ready to be shown around and that nobody was going to see it until it was ready. A little artistic temperament didn't bother him as long as he got the first reading when the script was done."

I remembered the stall, even though I hadn't spotted it as a stall at the time.

"I told Paddy the whole sad story, bloody glove and all. He already knew about me and Ted. That surprised me."

It didn't surprise me, given my recent conversation with Captain Grove. Nor was I surprised that Paddy had never told me, given my long relationship with him.

Ella seemed to address my thoughts. "Paddy advised me not to say anything to you. He said something about the sanctity of the confessional. He told me to keep stalling Ted and let him handle everything.

"And he did. It wasn't more than a week later that Paddy brought me the glove. We burned it together."

I had no trouble picturing that scene, as I'd participated in a dress rehearsal featuring Rosa Mariutto.

Again, Ella seemed to be reading my mind. "Paddy said you'd played a big part in getting that glove back."

"A bit part, he meant," I said. "My standard part."

I flipped the bread and the bread circles, using a spatula that was a long lost friend. Then I put a pat of butter into each of the holes. By the time I got the first egg cracked, the butter had melted. I dropped the egg into one of the holes, being careful not to break the yoke. Then I repeated the procedure on slices two and three.

"How did you deal with Mariutto?"

"I never had to. Paddy told me that I could never let on that I knew Ted had lost the glove. If he tried to bluff me, I was to play the temperamental artist again. I was to say that nothing was more important to me than *Private Hopes* getting its due. I was to tell Ted to go to the police if he wanted to. In fact, I was to promise to go to the police myself, if Ted ever threatened me again.

"Luckily, it never came to that. I sold *Private Hopes* to Dore Schary at Metro, and he issued a big press release. I never heard another peep from Ted."

I flipped two of the bread slices again, leaving the third untouched for Ella, who liked hers sunny-side up. We'd taken her story as far as I wanted to for the moment. Any farther and neither of us would feel like eating. So I decided to change the subject. The MIA bracelet, now safe in my pocket, had proven to be great for that when I'd had my talk with Grove, but I knew it would kill the present mood completely. I was still holding the familiar spatula, so I used it instead.

"I think this is mine. I seem to recall my mother giving it to me when I left Indiana."

"So you could paddle your canoe down the Wabash, probably," Ella replied. "That spatula came south with me from Sacramento. You can still see the Weinstock's Department Store name on the handle, if you've got your magnifying glass handy."

"Not that kind of detective," I said.

By then, I had the eggs on plates and Ella at the kitchen table. I even got her to eat a few mouthfuls. We ate in silence, our old companionable silence, until she noticed another adjustment I'd made to my personal jewelry.

"You're not wearing your wedding ring. I didn't think to look the last time you were here. Gabby said you still wear it."

"We certainly named her right," I said.

"I hope you didn't take it off because you thought I'd ask for it back."

"It is fourteen carat."

I hated to break the spell, but the clock was ticking and Ella had given me an opening. "Speaking of Gabby," I said, "why did her telling you about the Mariutto operation upset you so much? It's ancient history."

"It should be," Ella said, "but somehow it's not. When Paddy found that glove, he missed the affidavit of a woman who saw me leave the Sea Hawk the night of the murder. Paddy found it ten years later—I'm not sure where—and brought it to me.

"That was right after the Johnny Remlinger business. I was still in shock from that. Paddy promised me he'd destroy the affidavit, and I let him."

"That's still ancient history."

"Wait. About a month ago, just before Paddy was killed, he phoned me. He wanted to warn me that a copy of the affidavit had turned up. He said he was going to find out about it. He was going to settle things once and for all.

"I asked him not to. I told him the affidavit without the glove was worthless. He told me not to worry. 'Don't worry a hair on your head' was how he put it. Then you called to say he was dead."

CHAPTER TWENTY-EIGHT

Ella got up from the table and went out onto her back porch. It had a million-dollar view, like Amos Decker's, and ran the width of the house, like Decker's, but it was only about three strides deep, just deep enough to hold a few potted plants and the café table and chairs that Ella ignored on her walk to the metal railing.

I joined her there, touching Ella's shoulder with mine. I didn't want her to put any distance between us again, the real kind of distance or the really dangerous kind. I thought it was my turn in the witness box, that Ella was about to ask me the question I'd dodged earlier: Why had I shown up that day? But she wasn't through herself.

"I'm sorry I didn't come to you and tell you everything when Paddy was killed," she said. "I was too ashamed to."

"Ashamed of what? You tried to warn him off."

"Ashamed that my old sins got him killed. It was Billy all over again. In my darker moments, I used to think Billy had picked up my guilt the way he got my blue eyes, in the womb, and that what happened to him happened because of me."

"Ella—"

"I know, Scotty, it's a crazy idea. A woman with doctor in front of her name and half the alphabet behind it told me that once a week for about a year. Finally, I believed her. But when Paddy died, I felt it all over again, the shame. I couldn't come to you and confess everything. Couldn't even hold your hand at Paddy's funeral. I'm so sorry.

"I'd almost worked through it when you showed up Tuesday to tell me you were helping Amos Decker resurrect the Mariutto con. I knew then what it feels like to believe in an unforgiving god or karma or fate or whatever name you want to give to the realization you're chained at the ankle to every bad thing you ever did.

"I should have warned you off that day, but I couldn't."

"You tried," I said.

"That's why I came to Malibu last night, to try again."

"I'm sorry you missed me." Sincerely sorry, although I was pretty sure an alibi provided by me would carry no weight at all with Grove. "I'd like to use the confessional now, if you're done with it."

Ella thought we were still on the subject of ancient romances. "What is it, Scotty? Were you one of the men in Mary Astor's diary?"

There was a smile in her voice I hadn't heard in a long time. I hoped I'd hear it again when we made it to the other side of this.

I said, "That knock on the door you've been waiting for could come at any time. I drove here last night to tell you that I knew about you and Mariutto and the glove and how Paddy had gotten you off the hook in '52.

"I let you tell me the whole story just now because I wanted you to and because I think you needed to. Some of what you told me I didn't know, like what Mariutto was after with his blackmail play. The rest I'd worked out or guessed at."

"How?"

"I found my way to the woman who gave Paddy the deposition. Her name was Helen Gallimore. She was Sugar Stapert's sister."

"Was?" Ella said, not even the ghost of a smile in her voice now.

"Somebody shot her last night, while I was here and you were in Malibu."

"While I claim to have been in Malibu," Ella said, cutting right to the point. "I'll never be able to prove I was there."

"Maybe we can. Maybe it won't come to that. At the moment, there's no way for the police to get from Gallimore to you. The murderer took away the last copies of the deposition."

"Why would he do that, Scotty? Why would anybody but me do that?"

"That's what we have to figure out before the police come calling on you or me or both of us."

I handed Ella my copy of the deposition.

"This is just how I remember it from '62," she said. "It's all about the glove and nothing without the glove. What could Paddy have seen in this?"

"Agnes Brown's name and address, for one thing. And something Brown said in passing. It's right here. 'I expected to see one of the boys who were always mooning around Miss Stapert.'"

"When I talked to Rosa Wardell, your stand-in during Paddy's con, she called Stapert a mantrap. You just said pretty much the same thing, that she always had men hanging around her."

"She did," Ella said. "It was wartime. There were always a lot of servicemen hanging around Los Angeles, waiting to be shipped out."

"There was one other thing the killer took from Gallimore's. In her bedroom, she had a photo of her sister. I think it's in his bedroom now."

"My God," Ella said.

"I think what Paddy saw was the possibility of another suspect, one of Stapert's old hangers on."

"How could he have hoped to find one of those after thirty years?"

"Through Agnes Brown, if she's still alive and if he could trace her. We know Paddy found the answer, so we know it's out there to find."

"We know it was," Ella said. "It may not be now. If someone followed Paddy's trail back to Gallimore and killed her, he could have done the same thing to Agnes Brown."

I hadn't thought of that. I elected not to, for the moment.

"I'm more worried about following Paddy's trail myself. So far, I haven't been able to. I've got the whole agency trying to trace Agnes. They're also collecting old newspaper stories about the Stapert murder."

I was still holding my shoulder tight against Ella's. I felt hers jerk suddenly, as though I'd handed her a worn electric cord.

"I have some of those," she said. She hurried back inside the house, and I followed her like my name was on the deed.

She led me into a part of the house I hadn't visited, her bedroom. Terra incognito, Gabrielle might have called it. It was as plain as Gabby had described it, but that wasn't what made my heart sink. It was the bedroom's resemblance to the room where Helen Gallimore had died, right down to the little shrine of photographs on the otherwise bare dresser. There were again three photos in linked frames, like an ancient altarpiece. The two flanking photos were of Gabby and Billy, both taken in grade school. The middle photo was one Ella and I had posed for on our wedding day.

Ella ignored the shrine and me as she dug in a long drawer, finally pulling out what I would have mistaken for a drawer liner if I'd been casually poking around. In fact, I might have mistaken the yellowed newsprint for that more than once, if Ella had had the sheets the whole time we'd been married.

"You have these why?"

"I thought I might write about it someday," Ella said. "Either as therapy or to try to make sense of it. To tell the truth, I'd forgotten I had them until Paddy called about the affidavit copy. Since he was killed, I've been afraid to touch them."

She was still afraid of them, to judge by the way she shoved them at me. I carried them to the table where we'd had our eggs.

"If you'd gotten around to writing it," I said on the way, "how would you have worked out the murder?"

Ella thought it over, running a hand through her short hair while she did. "I guess I would have leaned the way you're leaning, toward a Mr. boyfriend."

"You never thought Mariutto might have done it?"

"Not really. Ted was nine kinds of louse, but I couldn't see him killing anybody."

I was a little tired of her calling Mariutto "Ted." She made up for it somewhat by adding, "He didn't have the sand."

The loose sheets of newsprint were all from the *Los Angeles Examiner*. Ella had arranged them by date, which didn't surprise me. The first mention of the murder was a front-page story, but it was a single paragraph below the fold that didn't even give the victim's name. The upper portion of the same sheet was devoted to official communiqués on a big naval battle fought off the Philippines a week or so earlier and an article about the run-up to FDR's reelection.

The second "Sea Hawk Murder" story gave Stapert's stage name but not her real one. It also mentioned her age, twenty-two, and the fact that she'd been shot to death. According to the paper, she'd been found by workers coming to open the club a little after noon, by which time she'd been dead for hours. No mention of the club's owners, either the public one, Errol Flynn, or the private one, Mariutto. No mention of any love interest for Stapert, in fact. The story was squeezed between a long one about famine in Greece and a smaller one on a place in Germany where the army was bogged down but expected to "punch through soon," the "Hürtgen Forest."

Significantly, I thought, the third story didn't run until several days after that. The Sea Hawk Murder tag, which was the kind of thing journalists assigned a story with staying power, was gone, as was Stapert's name. In fact, the third story was almost a rewording of the first, early bulletin, the only addition a sad one: "The police have no leads."

The police had one now, I thought, though I was hoping they didn't realize it. I said, "The fix really was in. The *Examiner* couldn't drop the story fast enough."

"I'd forgotten how short they were," Ella said. "I guess my guilty conscience has been fleshing them out. They're really no more use than the affidavit."

"Together they might be of some use," I said. "The fact that they contradict one another might be. Agnes Brown said Stapert always had men mooning around her. In the newspaper stories, she might've been a nun."

"Ted's name was left out because his mob friends told somebody to leave it out. But why didn't they mention any of the other men in her life?"

"Exactly," I said. "It could've been because at least one of the others was so close to Mariutto he was covered by his mob protection policy. Did you know Little Al Alsip?"

"Yes, though he was part of the crowd Ted tried to keep me

away from. He drove Ted around from time to time, so I knew him by sight. Why?"

"Rosa Wardell, who was once Rosa Mariutto, told me that Alsip was one of Sugar Stapert's conquests. I've asked Ed Sharpe to find him. I may try it myself. If you've got Alsip tucked away in another drawer, tell me now."

"Sorry," Ella said and started to gather her newspaper sheets. "I did see Alsip once a few years ago, though. You were with me."

"Where was that?"

"Lake Arrowhead. We were borrowing Ruth Hussey's cabin for the weekend."

"I remember the weekend," I said.

"I saw Alsip in town, near the inn. He didn't see me. He was standing next to a tow truck and wearing the uniform that went with it. I didn't point him out to you because . . ."

"Right," I said. "Feel like a drive? I'd like to see Ruth's cabin again."

CHAPTER TWENTY-NINE

We'd borrowed Ruth Hussey's cabin in 1968, during the last untroubled months of our marriage, which made our chances of finding Al Alsip in residence in Lake Arrowhead in 1974 no better than the odds on a trifecta. But there were other reasons for making the drive. One was to get Ella and me out of the jurisdiction of the LAPD for a while. For as long as it took Hollywood Security to locate Agnes Brown, I hoped.

Another good reason was to give us a little more time in the bubble of our old life together that had somehow formed around us. I didn't expect it to last any longer than any other bubble—certainly not if policemen started poking it—but while it lasted, I was speaking and walking softly.

And driving carefully. Once we were down off Ella's mountain ridge, the route was almost all freeway. I chose the northernmost freeways, the ones farthest from Helen Gallimore and the mess she'd started. That meant picking up the Colorado Freeway, which they were now calling the Ventura, in the San Fernando Valley and sticking with it until it became the road that skirted the San Gabriel Mountains, the Foothill Freeway.

Somewhere around San Dimas, Ella said, "You can put it back on, if you want. Your wedding band."

"Thanks," I said and dug in my pocket for it. I was careful not to bang it against the copper bracelet that I also carried there, but that was careful wasted.

"The MIA bracelet, too, if you like," Ella added.

I was thinking that, if I wanted to be near my wife again, I'd just have to put up with the extrasensory perception, when she explained it away.

"Gabby told me about it, too. She's thinking of ordering one for herself. I think she'll have an engagement ring first."

That was more than an attempt by Ella to change the subject she'd brought up herself and now regretted. It was news to me and big news. Ella told me then about Gabrielle's "young man," a senior at UCLA named Sven. Gabby might have told me herself the night I found her at the beach house, if I hadn't shown up bruised and battered and preoccupied with a long dead con game.

The telling took us to San Bernardino, where we traded the freeway for a winding, ridgeline two-lane. At Crestline, we traded down again to the little road that served the towns between Lake Gregory and Lake Arrowhead.

We were creeping through Blue Jay when it occurred to me that, by taking Ella beyond Grove's reach and into Alsip's, I might be moving her from the frying pan to the fire. That assumed that Alsip was the killer, that he still lived in Lake Arrowhead, and that he'd retreated there after killing Gallimore. I told myself that of those three dubious assumptions, the third was the least likely. If Little Al had found Gallimore through me, he was probably lying in wait for me in LA right now, as Ed Sharpe had predicted. That conclusion caused me to ask a seemingly unrelated question.

"Where is Gabrielle this weekend?"

"Visiting Sven's family."

"In Stockholm, by any chance?"

"Santa Barbara."

Ella didn't comment further until we were pulling into Lake Arrowhead Village. Then she said something that had me thinking of ESP all over again: "If you brought along a gun, I won't make my usual objections."

"Duly noted."

"How will you find him?"

"I was hoping you'd remember the name on the side of his tow truck."

"Sorry. Not even the color of the truck. Where do we start?"

"Where every experienced investigator starts. With the phone book."

We parked next to the old dance pavilion, whose conical roof and church steeple spire made it the most prominent local landmark. The rest of the village's architecture was strictly Swiss chalet meets Hollywood set designer. In the black-timbered inn, I found my phone book. I checked for Alsip's name in the white pages with little hope and less luck. Then I started a list of towing services and garages, using a pad and pencil from Ella's purse.

"When Tory Beaumont played a private eye, he just tore out the directory page," Ella said, worrying the desk clerk who'd lent me the book, a very pale redhead not many years out of pigtails.

To reassure the clerk, I made small talk. "We noticed some placards posted around for a referendum. What's that all about?"

"The new dam," she said. "The old one won't stand up to an earthquake, they say. Like that dam that almost caved in down south during the last big quake."

"The Van Norman Dam," said Ella, who, like me and the rest of Los Angeles, had been too close to that quake for comfort.

"Right. We either build a new damn or lower the lake level seventy feet. We'd all be out of work then. So it's pay up now or pay up later."

"It always is," Ella told her.

I didn't like the sound of that, but Ella didn't retreat back into her shell. When we reached our car, she leaned against its landau roof, examined my list, and said, "Not many places to check. We could have done this by phone."

"And missed the view?"

I meant the glittering lake and the pine-forested hills and the serious mountains beyond them. But my view also contained Ella, squinting at me over the Continental's roof, the sunlight making her narrowed eyes as blue as the water behind her.

"Pretty good from this side, too," she said.

Our first stop was a filling station at the edge of the village. The kid who pumped my gas was the whole staff on duty. He'd never heard of Alsip or seen anyone fitting his distinctive description. We did a little better at our next stop, a three-bay garage near the Saddle Inn. The mechanic we spoke to, whose eyes kept straying to the still youthful Ella in a way I didn't approve of but understood, remembered someone who might have been Alsip.

"Haven't seen him around in years. Heard he was sick or something. He never did look like he could count on his next breath. Or he went away or something. Ask at Ned's in Cedar Glen."

Ned's was on my list. It had advertised itself as both a garage and a marine engine shop in the Yellow Pages. Cedar Glen was on the lake's northern shore. In spite of its name, the dominant trees in the area were pines. They'd been part of the backdrop in Lake Arrowhead, but here they were a presence, their green-black branches filtering the light and the heat—making the windbreaker under which I'd hidden my holstered thirty-eight a little less unlikely—their needles dampening our footsteps as we climbed from the road where I'd parked to the cinderblock building.

There, in an open bay, we found a workman tearing down an outboard motor perched on a wooden stand. The mechanic was still in his twenties, if only just, with bushy sideburns and a frizzy, Gene Hackman comb-over. In place of overalls, he wore fatigues with USMC stenciled on one breast pocket.

His "Help you?" was directed at Ella, so she answered him, asking for Alsip by name, which produced a quizzical look, and then by description. That struck home.

"The world's oldest ten-year-old, I always called the little guy," the garageman said. "Al Smith was the name on his paychecks, same as the old-time politician."

Same last name as the one I'd used the day Alsip and I had played follow-the-leader through Beverly Hills, though that was surely a coincidence.

At that point we were joined by a man in the prime of his life, which is to say, my age. He'd been better fed than I had recently and carried his surplus in a gut supported by a big silver belt buckle. He wore half glasses and no hair worth combing over. Ned, I assumed.

"What's this?" he said gruffly. Even the sight of Ella didn't soften him, so he might have been older than I'd guessed.

"Asking about Al Smith, Mr. Prescott," the mechanic said.

"Why?"

I handed him a fancy business card, which he handed back, bent. I said, "We'd like to find him."

"So would I," Prescott said. "The little weasel left me flat. Left my sister-in-law's place owing a month's rent."

"This was when?"

"Years ago."

"Three years," the ex-Marine said, winning himself a dark look from his boss.

"How long had he been with you?"

"A while," Ned said and glowered at the mechanic, who went back to work. "That's all I can tell you, except he knew how to drive and change a tire. Good day."

We headed out but slowly, on the off chance Prescott would remember urgent business elsewhere. He didn't. But when we reached the open end of the bay, the mechanic called out to us.

"If you're looking for a good dinner place, try the Yellow Rose."

CHAPTER THIRTY

We next inquired at Cedar Glen's general store. The woman who owned the place remembered Al Smith and his sudden departure but claimed not to have much interest in it, as she'd never extended Smith credit. That comment reminded me of Prescott's sister-in-law who rented rooms. The general store owner directed us to her house. We rang the bell there and knocked and got no answer. So either the landlady was out or she'd been forewarned by her sociable brother-in-law.

My next stop would normally have been the nearest police station or sheriff's substation, but I couldn't be sure our names and descriptions wouldn't be hot off a Teletype, courtesy of Captain Grove. So we drove back to Lake Arrowhead.

"Why do you suppose that motorboat repairman recommended a restaurant to us?" Ella asked as we followed the lakeshore.

"For a kickback, I guess. In a city, restaurants pay off cabbies and hotel doorman. Up here, they pay off motorboat repairmen and maybe lumberjacks."

"Scotty."

"Okay, I suppose he recommended the Yellow Rose for the same reason you're supposing. But if we hang around to find out, we'll get back pretty late."

"It would make more sense to stay the night," Ella said.

"Yes," I said. "It would."

We checked in to the Saddle Inn. I asked for two rooms and

waited for Ella to correct me. She didn't. I asked that they be connecting rooms and waited for Ella to object. She didn't.

She went off to buy toothbrushes and other supplies while I placed a call to Hollywood Security. To my own direct line, to be specific. Vickie answered, as I hoped she would. So far, the operatives she'd pulled off paying jobs hadn't traced Agnes Brown. But someone was trying to trace me, Captain Grove. So my half-day's grace was gone with the wind. Vickie closed her report with a question.

"Do you want to speak with Mr. McLean?"

"I don't know," I said. "Do I?"

"You do not," Vickie said.

"So long, then."

Ella hadn't come back, so I canvassed local businesses for people who remembered Al Smith. I collected a couple of vague memories of a little man who never spoke and one bit of cryptic testimony. It came from a shopkeeper who was giving up for the day. I caught her as she was unlocking her Pinto.

"Al Smith? Little guy? Blond hair that was almost white? Wasn't he the guy they were calling 'the laddie in the lake'?"

She laughed at that until she was safely locked in her car and rolling away. I noted the name of her antique shop, in case Ella and I were wrong about the mechanic's dinner advice. Then I made a point of finding the Yellow Rose.

It was a big place for that small a town, a rambling ranch house whose exterior design featured wagon wheels and whose shake-shingled roof had drifts of pine needles so deep they were sprouting baby trees.

The place opened at five for happy hour, and Ella I were there shortly afterwards, nursing longnecks at the bar.

"Instead of toothbrushes," I said, "you should've bought us ten-gallon hats."

"You're just sore because they don't have any Duke Ellington records in the jukebox."

"I'd settle for Spike Jones. I don't remember this place from our last visit, but it must have been here. It must have been here for the gold rush."

"Cowboy bars are the coming thing," Ella said. "We'll have them in LA before too long. You'll be rooting for disco then."

"I'll be rooting for the next earthquake then."

A new song started playing on the jukebox, a popular one, if the number of couples who headed for the dance floor was any indication. Ella took my hand.

"Come on, cowboy. They're playing our song."

I didn't argue, even though our song had always been "I'll Get By." The name of this one, to judge by the chorus, was "World of Make Believe," so Ella might have been onto something. I know she was as light in my arms as she'd been the first time we'd danced, and she was nestled just as close. And given our recent history and the spot we were in, that felt a lot like make believe.

The Saturday night crowd was grabbing up tables, so we traded the bar for one of the last open ones. To pass the time, I told Ella about the rumors that had circulated in the LAPD after Ted Mariutto had driven himself into a canyon, rumors about some mobster arranging it.

Ella said, "Poor Ted," and I let it pass.

I moved us on instead to my theory that it might have been Alsip who'd shown Mariutto the door. Ella said nothing to that, and I got around to noticing that she'd stopped listening. I followed her gaze and saw that the leatherneck mechanic had arrived.

In addition to getting crowded, the Yellow Rose had gotten noisy and dark, which may have been the atmosphere our contact had been waiting for. He picked up a beer at the bar and then wandered our way. His off-duty attire was jeans and a Western shirt, complete with piping across its shoulders and pocket flaps. He nodded at our spare chair, and Ella nodded back.

"Spotted your MIA bracelet back at the shop," he said to me. He extended his arm, displaying a bracelet of his own, in silver.

"I didn't notice that earlier," I said.

"Don't wear it at work. Can't even wear a wristwatch. Catch it on the wrong piece of an engine that's running, and my arm would be MIA."

He gave his wrist a gentle shake. "This is for a buddy of mine from Camp Pendleton. We were sent to Vietnam as replacements and ended up in different outfits. He never came home."

He didn't ask after the history of mine, luckily, perhaps

assuming that I was carrying around a stranger's name, as many people did. Instead, he extended a big hand. "Ben Travois."

I introduced myself and Ella. That got Travois' sleepy eyes fully open. "Husband-and-wife detectives? I thought that only happened in the movies."

"That's where Scotty gets all his best ideas," Ella said. "Was there something you wanted to tell us about Al Smith?"

"Yes, ma'am. I mean, I wanted to tell you that you won't hear much about Al from the locals. There's a kind of unwritten law around here against anything that could hurt the tourist business, including any kind of gossip that could hurt it. That goes double if the gossip concerns the lake itself. Biggest stretch of holy water you ever saw, that lake.

"This whole referendum thing has been a revelation to me. In the old days, they would've fixed it on the q.t., but I guess you can't build a new dam when nobody's looking."

"How about sinking somebody in the lake when nobody's looking?" I asked. "Is that what happened to Al Smith?"

"That's one popular theory. I guess I should back us up a ways. Al was working at the shop when I got home from 'Nam. Old Ned had saved a place for me in the garage, but he'd taken on Al as a driver. Anyway, all we knew about Al was that he'd come up from Los Angeles and he'd been a driver, maybe for somebody in the movie business. I thought he might've come up here for his health—his chest was about as big around as my thigh—but when I suggested that to him, he just gave a little laugh. Only laugh I ever heard out of him. The laugh and the way he watched his back made me think he was hiding from something.

"Whatever it was caught up to him in the fall of '71. He didn't show up for work one day and wasn't at the room he rented. We found his car parked at the foot of an old gravel boat ramp that's not used much anymore. No sign of Al himself. Never has been any sign. Ned Prescott and the others I call 'town elders' decided that Al had just gone away, maybe faking a suicide to cover his trail. Other people think he's in the lake. These cold mountain lakes, they don't give up their bodies so easy."

"What do you think, Ben?" Ella asked.

Travois drank off his beer with a flourish. "I think if the

referendum fails and they have to lower the lake as much as they're saying, we may see Al again."

It wasn't that late when we got back to the Saddle Inn, but Ella said good night immediately. I'd felt all day that I'd been pushing my luck with her, so I didn't argue. I did unlock my side of the connecting door, in case trouble visited us in the night. And I placed my gun on the nightstand. Then I settled in to watch my room's television, a portable with weak vertical hold that could just pick up a single San Bernardino station.

A little after ten, the deadbolt snapped back on Ella's side of the connecting door. I was reaching for the thirty-eight when the door opened, revealing Ella, wearing only her blue blouse, and that buttoned in the Sugar Stapert manner.

For a moment, she just stood in the doorway. Then she said, "A screenwriter friend of mine once told me that if your plot hits a dead-end, you should have a man enter carrying a gun."

"I like your approach better," I said.

CHAPTER THIRTY-ONE

We took our time heading out on Sunday morning. I spent part of that time trying to talk Ella into staying behind in Lake Arrowhead. I told her she'd be safer and I'd be happier. Her counterargument, which I couldn't answer, was to take my arm and hold on.

The interior of the Lincoln had seemed like a very intimate space on the drive up. On the drive south, the lounge seats were way too far apart. As we drove, we debated the subject that had divided the Cedar Glen gossips, the Al Alsip question. It really was a debate, as we found ourselves on opposing sides. I got us started by suggesting that Alsip had staged his disappearance in '71 and returned to Los Angeles.

"Why, Scotty? If some old enemies of Ted's chased Alsip up here, why would he ever go back? It's not like he could hope to blend in."

"Like I was trying to tell you last night, the LAPD thinks the mob might have arranged Mariutto's accident. I think they're wrong. I think it was the same guy who killed Stapert and Paddy and Gallimore. And that guy could be Little Al."

Ella echoed Ed Sharpe then. "Why would Alsip kill Ted? He worshiped him."

"Maybe he didn't like his severance package. Maybe Mariutto knew that Alsip had killed Stapert and he was holding it over his head. When Alsip heard Morrie Bender was finally dead, he knew he could come after Mariutto without fear of reprisals. He slipped down to LA, killed his old boss, and then went back to driving his tow truck in Cedar Glen. He kept at it until he was sure the police weren't treating Mariutto's death as a murder. Then he staged his own disappearance and came back to town."

"Why stage a disappearance?" Ella asked. "That only drew attention to himself. Why didn't he just hand in his notice and pay his back rent and leave? The town would have forgotten him by now. And even if he did sneak away, how do you know we went back to LA? He could have gone anywhere."

"Paddy died in LA," I reminded her.

But her objection had also reminded me of something. Sharpe had told me about Alsip dropping out of sight when Mariutto let him go. He hadn't said a word about Alsip popping up again. I didn't give Ella that ammunition. She didn't need it.

"I think Ben Travois was right," she said. "Alsip was at Lake Arrowhead hiding from someone. And that someone finally tracked him down. You're always finding clues in movies, Scotty. I'm surprised you haven't mentioned *Out of the Past*. Robert Mitchum is a garage owner whose old mob employers catch up with him."

"How about *The Killers*?" I asked. "Burt Lancaster is a gas station attendant who's spotted by one of his old stickup gang and gets rubbed out. Garage workers with shady pasts seemed to have been a film noir subgenre."

"That has to have been how it happened," Ella said. "Some visitor to Lake Arrowhead spotted Alsip the same way I did and word got around back in Los Angeles. When it got to the wrong person—Sugar Stapert's killer if you're right—he came for Alsip."

"Why? What threat was he?"

"Maybe Alsip knew the truth about who killed Sugar. He and Ted both. Once Morrie Bender was dead, the killer took them both out to protect himself.

"It's the simplest explanation, Scotty. You don't have to explain Alsip going back and forth to LA. The real killer never left LA. And Alsip really is in that lake. So you don't have the problem of explaining why he staged his disappearance."

"If Alsip's in that lake, I have a bigger problem. I've lost my only suspect in Helen Gallimore's murder—and Paddy's. Without Alsip, I'm back to square one."

That realization put us both in a brown study until Muscoy. Then Ella said, "How did Paddy manage to find Agnes Brown when the new Hollywood Security can't?"

"Because he knew a guy who knew a guy. He had more connections than Ma Bell. But he never shared one if he could avoid it. If he had, I'd know a guy who knows a guy."

Ella thought that over for as long as it took my odometer to click off a mile. "What kind of guy would that even be?" she asked then. "Did Paddy know somebody in the domestics' union? Who knows more than one housekeeper at a time?"

"Howard Johnson must know a few thousand."

"He's dead," Ella said, but by then I was braking hard. "Scotty, what is it?"

When I had us safely on the shoulder, I turned to face her. "Casper Wheeler."

"The Wheeler House guy? What about him?"

"He was at Paddy's funeral. He told me he'd seen Paddy recently. I was too numb that day to give it any thought, but why would he have seen him? How could he have?"

"Only if Paddy had been to see him," Ella said. "Wheeler's employed a lot of maids in his time. And he's a leader in the black community. If anyone could trace Agnes Brown, he could."

We stuck to the freeway as far as Rancho Cucamonga. There we headed south. We'd gone too far already in the Continental. Captain Grove surely had every cop in Los Angeles on the lookout for it. I drove us to the nearby and therefore confusingly named Ontario International Airport, and we left the Lincoln in its parking garage. Golden State Car Rental was long out of business, or I would have rented from them for old times' sake. We made do with Hertz and continued our drive in a plain, white Torino sedan.

That drive took us west again, this time on the Pomona Freeway, which deposited us in Los Angeles itself. The Wheeler House was on Central Avenue. It wasn't a tall building, but on its block of low-rise commercial properties, it was a landmark.

Half of the first floor of the Wheeler House was given over to its jazz club, the Amber Room. In its glory days, the room had hosted Louie Armstrong, Charles Parker, Shorty Rogers, and Dave Brubeck, to name just a few. Since the rock-and-roll tsunami had hit the coast, the whole Central Avenue jazz scene had suffered. Some clubs now hosted rock groups or groups that had one foot on the jazz dock and another in the rock canoe. So far, the Amber Room had held the line. We found Casper Wheeler there, auditioning a combo.

Wheeler took us into a small lounge off the main performance space, an empty lounge on that Sunday afternoon. It was decorated in dark red paper and mirrors tinted in gold. What light there was came from hanging lanterns with red shades that belonged in a Chinese restaurant.

Wheeler looked younger than he had at Paddy's funeral. He wasn't in morning sunlight, for one thing, and he'd traded his suit for a white polo shirt and dark slacks. He wore a pink silk scarf around his throat, tied tightly and tucked into his shirt's open neck.

Ella commented on the trio Wheeler had been auditioning as we settled into a booth near the kitchen door.

"I've always loved music," he said. "Really good music. It's a funny thing, 'cause I'm an equal threat on any instrument you can name. Can't play a one. But the first job I ever had was washing dishes in a club here on Central—the old Blue Hat—and I fell in love with the music. I moved out of the kitchen to wait tables just so I could hear more of it. That's the reason I started my own little place. And I only bought this hotel so I could have the Amber Room and make it the best jazz club on the coast.

"There was a time when all the top jazz players in the world came to me. Me, a guy who couldn't carry a tune. Funny how things worked out."

I'd been wondering how best to introduce the reason for our visit. Wheeler did it for me.

"Sorry, Scotty. I couldn't tell you. I wanted to. I thought you'd want to know. But Paddy made me swear I wouldn't. He said it wasn't safe for you to know. I've heard since that you've been looking for Paddy's killer. I would've known that without hearing about it, to be honest. I should've called you, but the way Paddy died, I knew he was right. It is too dangerous for you to know."

"It's more dangerous for me not to know."

"More dangerous for us," Ella added.

"For you, Miss Ella?"

"Paddy got involved in this in the first place because of me."

Wheeler was still on the fence. I understood that. If Paddy had extracted a promise from me on his last day, I'd still be keeping it on mine. I tried to nudge Wheeler by giving up the rest of what we knew.

"Paddy came to you for help. He wanted to find a woman named Agnes Brown. In 1944, she worked as a cleaning woman at the Sea Hawk, a club in San Pedro. A singer named Sugar Stapert was murdered there, and Agnes knew something about it. Whatever she knew, she told Paddy."

"Yes." Wheeler gave up the single word like it had roots as deep as his heart. "But she's not going to tell it to you. She knows what happened to Paddy. She doesn't want to end up in an alley herself."

"Then she'd better talk to me today. Did Paddy tell you how he heard about Agnes?"

"He showed me a sworn statement from Agnes. I don't know where he got it."

"Sugar Stapert's sister gave it to him. She's been here in Los Angeles since the fifties, looking for her sister's killer. The killer found her two days ago. She had other copies of the deposition Agnes gave back in '44. He took those with him. So he's not just a threat to Ella and me. Sooner or later, he'll come for Agnes, too. And my guess is it will be sooner. Has anyone else been asking for her?"

"No," Wheeler said. "Not that I've heard."

"But she's in Los Angeles."

"Yes."

"Ever since the war?"

"Yes. Moved up from San Pedro and got married to a man who'd been in the service. When he died, she married again. She hasn't been hiding or covering her tracks. There's been no reason for her to. She's an honest woman and always has been. But, like I told Paddy, some people live lightly on this earth. They make their own way and keep to themselves. They don't need the government and they don't bother the law. They don't bother anyone."

"It isn't right that this thing should have come to Agnes."

"No," I said. "It's not."

I didn't add that this thing had come to Paddy, too, and in a big way. I couldn't claim that Paddy had lived lightly on the earth. Or that he'd been an innocent victim. As Gabrielle had observed, he'd gone looking for what he'd found.

Wheeler said, "This has come to Agnes because of me. Nothing would have happened if I hadn't put Paddy in touch with her. This is my fault. Guess I should try to put it right."

He settled back in his padded seat, suddenly looking every day of his age. "I heard her sing once, Sugar Stapert. At an after-hours jam session right here on the avenue. I remember thinking, 'Sings like an angel, looks like a devil.'

"I'll make a call."

CHAPTER THIRTY-TWO

We ate a late lunch right there in the booth in the Amber Room's lounge, Casper Wheeler playing waiter, as he'd once done at the old Blue Hat. He might have been feeling nostalgic. Ella certainly was. She was holding my hand and smiling like we didn't have a care in the world.

"You're in a good mood," I observed.

"I know. If I were writing a screenplay about a broken couple getting back together and on the run to boot, one or both of them would be crying on every other page. I don't feel like crying. I feel like I've caught a break whatever happens."

"Whatever happens," I said.

When Wheeler came back, he was all business. "Agnes will see you. Just you," he added, apologizing to Ella with a sidelong glance. "You'll be picked up in five minutes. They don't want to give you time to set up a tail."

"They?"

"Agnes's nephews. She never had any kids herself, but she married into a big family. Be careful around them, Scotty. They love their aunt."

"I will be."

"Oh, I'd better take that gun you're carrying under your jacket."

I handed him the thirty-eight, belt holster and all.

Wheeler gave it a close look, weighing it in his hand as he did.

"This looks like the gun Paddy left with me."

"It is the gun," I said.

"Glad you're not superstitious. Come on."

"I'll meet you in the lobby," I said.

"Okay," Wheeler said. "But say good-bye fast."

Ella was on her feet, holding me the way she had at her front door. "We'd better not be saying good-bye."

"Casper will look after you till I get back."

"I think I'd rather go home and wait, Scotty."

"That wouldn't be safe. Just stay here."

"How long?"

"Give me two hours. Then call this number." I wrote Ed Sharpe's name and phone number on a cocktail napkin. A private eye's standard notepaper.

Ella knew Sharpe. "I think I should call him right now, Scotty. Or Captain Grove. I can handle him. He's always been afraid of me."

"You represent domesticity. Grove's allergic."

"Seriously, Scotty. We should be using the police, not hiding from them. We're playing into the killer's hand."

"We'll talk it over when I get back."

When I reached the hotel's one-sofa lobby, it was me and a potted palm and no Wheeler. Then I spotted him through the glass of the revolving door. He was at the curb, waving to me. Idling next to him was a mid-sixties Mercury Park Lane with windows tinted like a welder's goggles. As I stepped onto the sidewalk, the sedan's back door opened and a man got out. He was as big around at the waistband as Paddy had been in his heyday and bigger everywhere else.

He nodded me into the backseat, which was occupied on its far side by a man who appeared to be the first guy's big brother. I thought the nephew behind me would walk around to the front seat, which currently held only a driver, but he pushed in behind me instead, the arrangement effectively pinning my arms to my sides.

As soon as Wheeler slammed the door, the car took off. Our driver, who wore an afro the size of a space cadet's helmet, drove quickly, but without any sense of purpose. That is, we didn't seem to be in a hurry to get anywhere, making turns that undid prior turns and covering the same worn streets over and over again. So he really did have a purpose, which was to spot a car tailing us, in case I'd set that up in advance.

When we finally settled on a steady course, it took us farther south and a little east, into Watts. Almost ten years had gone by since the big riots, but here and there scars are still visible in the form of a boarded-up business too fire damaged to reopen. We pulled up in front of one of those and the largest I'd seen, a movie theater. The Rio Alhambra, according to its rusting marquee.

I was hustled out of the car and through the theater's front door, which contained more plywood than glass. The lobby we'd entered was dark. So dark that I felt more than saw the pat down I got. So dark that I didn't brace myself for the roundhouse to the stomach that doubled me over. It was just the one punch, meant to focus my attention on the voice that rasped in my ear.

"If anything happens to her, you're a dead man."

A second voice came from out of the darkness, not whispering. "Calvin, you stop that right now!"

I was still bent over, fighting to draw breath. When the lights came on, I saw them first as bright circles on the lobby's tile floor. One of the circles came my way. It was the beam of a powerful flashlight. It stayed focused on my shoes until I straightened. Then it hit me in the face. By then the second circle was shining on a figure seated in a folding chair.

She was small and stick thin and dressed for church. Her thinness and the angle of the second flashlight, which cast her eyes and sunken cheeks in shadow, gave her small head the appearance of a skull that happened to be topped by a pink gumdrop hat. Like me she was wearing unseasonable outerwear, in her case a wrapper as long and white as a lab coat.

I had enough wind by then for pleasantries. "Pleased to meet you, Mrs. . . ."

"Agnes will do fine. Mr. Wheeler said you used to be Mr. Maguire's man."

"Still am," I said. My back found a wall, and I leaned against it gratefully. "I want to find his killer. I think the same person may be after you."

"Mr. Wheeler said that, too. Because of the statement I put my name to for Ted Mariutto."

"You remember the statement?"

"I should. It was my way out of San Pedro. The money Mr. Mariutto paid me for it was my way out."

"Mariutto wanted you out of San Pedro. He wanted you where the police couldn't find you."

"I know that. I knew it at the time. I knew it was wrong."

Agnes let out a sigh that was half sob. In the darkness to my right, a big man shifted his feet on the gritty floor. This time, I did brace myself for a punch. It never came.

Instead, Agnes said, "Tell me about Mr. Maguire."

"Paddy?"

"Was he a good man?"

Take him all in all, I thought, falling back on an ancient hedge.

"He was definitely a great man," I said. "There wasn't a door in this town his name wouldn't open once. But he was a good man, too, I believe. A good friend to a lot of people, including me.

"If you're blaming yourself for getting him killed, don't. He did that to himself. A man whose name opens doors misses that when it's gone." Misses it more than the money or cigars or the primo banquettes at Romanoff's. "He wanted one more headline for bringing in Sugar Stapert's killer. That's what got him shot."

I'd come over to Grove's way of thinking on that. As Ella had pointed out, the deposition had been no real threat to her. But for Paddy it had been one last shot at a brass ring. I still didn't know why he'd wanted that ring badly enough to go into a dark alley looking for it.

"Thank you," Agnes said. "What do you want to know?"

"I want to know what Paddy asked you. Was it about the other men in Stapert's life, the ones you said were always hanging around her?"

"Yes. He thought one of them must have killed her. He said he knew the woman I'd seen leaving the club didn't do it. He didn't say how he knew.

"I didn't want to tell him about Miss Sugar's gentlemen. Not because I thought there was any harm in telling. Just because I was brought up not to speak ill of the dead. And Miss Sugar was my friend. She was from Mississippi, like I was. Talking to her mornings was like a visit home. I was lost and scared out here in

California, but Miss Sugar wasn't. She was sure she was going to own the whole state someday.

"I'd see her when I started my shift some mornings. She'd of just finished hers and be too keyed up to sleep. More often, though, she'd be sneaking in around the time I finished. I brought her a cup of coffee once, and she told me to go back and get one for myself. After that we talked regular. I guess she liked to hear a voice from home, too."

Agnes had been looking over my right shoulder as she thought back, as near as I could tell with the flashlight shining in my face. Now she turned her shadowy eyes to me.

"Mr. Wheeler said Miss Sugar's sister came out here looking for her killer and got killed herself. Is that so?"

It was the *Reader's Digest* version of Gallimore's unhappy life, but no less true for that. "Yes."

"What was her name, her first name?"

"Helen."

"That's right. I remember Miss Sugar talking about her sister. The country mouse, she called her. Miss Sugar wasn't any kind of mouse. Not to her way of thinking. She thought the men she met were the mice. They were all on this earth to do things for her and take her places and jump when she said to. Even Mr. Ted. I told her she was wrong, that men were the cats and we were the mice. That's the way the world had always been and always would be. She just laughed.

"I told Mr. Maguire I didn't remember any of her gentlemen friends' names. Miss Sugar made up nicknames for them, usually, so I never heard their real ones. And I've forgotten most of the nicknames. I remember one because I felt sorry for the boy who went with it. He was one of the few I actually saw, because he would hang around for hours after Miss Sugar sang or wait around for her to come back from a date with some other fellow.

"He was a soldier boy who'd been sent home sick. He still looked sick, his uniform hanging off him like a hand-me-down. Miss Sugar would laugh at him, right to his face. I never liked that."

"What was his nickname?" I asked.

"Miss Sugar called him Coconut. I never knew why. The name never made any sense to me. A lot of the soldier boys came home as brown as berries, but not Coconut. His face was pasty white. And all pockmarked, too, from the sickness he'd had, poor boy.

"That was the last thing I told Mr. Maguire. About Coconut, I mean. It told him something. Does it tell something to you?"

"Yes," I said. "It does."

CHAPTER THIRTY-THREE

I didn't say anything more to Agnes Brown beyond thanking her and urging her to be careful. When I was back in the Park Lane and headed north, sandwiched in the backseat as before, I gave her nephews a more detailed warning, instructions to be used in the event of my death.

The driver, who was again dividing his attention between the street ahead of us and the street behind us, said, "This guy we're supposed to look out for, you know his name?"

I did, though I couldn't quite make myself believe it. Not even when that name answered a last nagging question: If Ella wasn't in danger, if the business wasn't personal for Paddy, why had he run such a risk in that alley? The answer was that, for Paddy, the business had been personal, even without Ella as the damsel in distress. Maybe not at first, when he'd allowed himself to be "hired" by Helen Gallimore on a whim, but later, after he'd spoken to Agnes Brown.

A large elbow dug into my ribs. "So what is it?"

"Captain Walter Grove of the LAPD."

Walter Grove, the man who'd been at the edge of the bright lights from the start, who'd first mentioned Sugar Stapert to me back in 1952, after he'd heard that Hollywood Security had designs on Ted Mariutto. Grove, the ex-soldier who fit the description Brown had given me of Stapert's lovesick suitor. Grove, the man who'd tailed me to Helen Gallimore's and killed her, not after following me around for weeks or days or even hours, but because I'd invited him to the last stop I'd made before going back to check on Gallimore: the Intersection Lounge.

The driver whistled.

"You know him?" I asked.

"Well enough to stay away from him without being told to by any honky."

"Aunt Agnes never said anything about a cop," the nephew on my right said.

"She never heard his last name," I reminded him, "the one that made sense of his nickname."

"Coconut Grove," the nephew on my left said.

Stapert's pun still worked thirty years on, at least for people who lived amongst the ruins of old Hollywood. The Ambassador Hotel's Cocoanut Grove had been Hollywood's first giant supper club and its greatest, a soundstage of a room with fake palm trees scattered around a fake Moorish town square, under phony stars in a navy blue ceiling. There'd been real stars at its tables every night in the old days and aspiring ones crowding the dance floor, hoping to be noticed, like Sugar Stapert and, once upon a time, me. Paddy had been a regular there during the war. The moment he'd heard Brown's description of Stapert's soldier beau and heard his nickname, Paddy would have known he had the killer. And not just any killer, either, but his own personal nemesis, the cop who'd quit his payroll and then haunted him down through the years.

When we pulled onto Central Avenue a few blocks from the hotel, our driver said, "Unmarked car watching Wheeler's."

"Watching a car parked in front," I said. "Mine."

It'd been careless of me to leave the Torino on the street. But I hadn't expected the police to tie it to me so quickly.

I said, "Turn at the next block and drop me."

The nephews did, without a parting "good luck" or "go to hell." The block held an old Rexall drugstore and that held an old wooden phone booth, the kind that had once been my home away from home. I used it to call Ed Sharpe. I got another cop, who sounded like a newer member of the squad. He asked me for a name.

"Patrick J. Maguire," I said, trying to sound big enough to fit it.

Sharpe came on a moment later, his voice conveying a

breeziness that was every bit as convincing as the stuffed monkeys that had hung from the Cocoanut Grove's palm trees. "Paddy. I hadn't expected to hear from you again."

"Or from me either," I said.

"No," Sharpe said. "Captain Grove's arranged for my phone to be answered for me. Makes me feel like the president or like somebody nobody trusts anymore. Come to think of it, since Watergate, they're pretty much the same thing. Where are you?"

"On my way back to the Wheeler House."

"Bad idea. Grove has the place staked out."

"Grove killed Paddy."

"You're crazy."

"Maybe, but it's still true. He also killed Helen Gallimore, after I led him to her."

"Why?"

"Because in 1944 he killed Gallimore's sister. That's why he took her picture from Gallimore's family shrine. Grove told me he was in the service in '44." Knee-deep in sons of Nippon. "Find out when he actually got home. His dates of service will be in his personnel file."

"I don't need to check any files. Grove and I both served under Stilwell in Burma. He went home on a stretcher early in '44. Nearly dead of smallpox. That's how his face got marked up."

"You sure?"

"I should be. I served out my time in that hellhole. I've been junior to Grove on the force ever since."

"Find someone senior to him. Tell him what I told you. Ella and I need to sit down with somebody Grove can't order around." Ella and I and every overpaid lawyer Hollywood Security could line up.

"Your wife's involved in this? Did she call me by any chance? I was told I got a call half an hour ago from a woman, but there was no message on my desk."

"Could Grove have gotten hold of it?"

"Bet your life. That's why he's having my phone answered."

"Get over to Wheeler's fast."

"Scotty, Grove can't do anything with two plainclothesmen out front. Let him bring you in. You'll get your hearing."

"We'd never make it."

I hung up and headed for the Wheeler House at a run. Not to the staked-out front door, but to the back, which I prayed wasn't watched. It was, but not by a cop. A dishwasher or someone disguised as one was holding up the building's back wall, squeezing the last few drags out of a cigarette stub.

As I passed him, he said, "You Elliott? Casper told me to stop you if you came this way. There's a cop inside. He's got your wife."

I started past him, and he grabbed my arm. "Something's not right about that cat. He's drunk or sick or—"

The sound of a gunshot came to us from somewhere inside. I took off running again, first through a kitchen where the day shift stood frozen in place, then out into the lounge where we'd interviewed Wheeler. The jazz lover was there, on his back, open-eyed. Ella was in the booth where I'd left her, Grove seated beside her. The revolver in his hand was not quite pointed at Ella, not quite pointed at me.

"I had to do it," Grove said. "He had a gun. You'd better pick it up."

As Wheeler's man in the alley had said, something wasn't right with Grove. I could tell that even in the half-light of the lounge. He was sitting stock-still, but his black eyes were hitting every corner of the room. His face was gray and glistening with sweat, as though his Burma bugs were at him again.

Beside him, Ella was also very still. She was staring down at Wheeler, seeing yet another victim of her sins. For that reason alone, I almost bent down for the gun.

When I didn't, Grove barked, "Did you hear me, Elliott? I said pick it up."

I looked down with an effort. The gun, Paddy's gun, lay at my feet. Why Wheeler had decided to face Grove with it, I didn't know. I never would know. I was more concerned right then with the way the gun was lying. The butt was pointing the wrong way, toward Grove.

"Had it in this belt at the small of his back," Grove said. "Damn movie trick. Pick it up. Secure the scene."

"Let Ella go," I said. "You don't want her to hear what we're going to say."

"I say again, you don't want to know," Grove growled at me.

It took me a beat to realize that he was back at the Intersection Lounge. That we were back there, chatting over drinks. Grove gave me a clue by glancing down at the MIA bracelet that dangled on my wrist.

"I knew she'd had a fling with Moose Mariutto, an unpunished murderer. I told Maguire."

"Moose wasn't unpunished," I said. "He died in a wrecked car at the bottom of a canyon. You pushed him over. When it was safe to, after Morrie Bender was gone. When you traced Al Alsip to Lake Arrowhead, you gave him the same push."

It'd been a mistake to use the back door. I should have run in through the front, dragging the stakeout team in after me. Or sent Wheeler's backdoor guard around to get them before I charged in.

"Alsip was a punk," Grove said. "He thought he had a chance with her, believe it or not." He looked at Ella then, confused, expecting to see someone else beside him.

"With Sugar Stapert?" I said to draw him back to me.

"Right. With Sugar."

"Why wouldn't Alsip have a chance with Stapert? Didn't every man? Every man but you, that is. She laughed at you. When you'd had your fill of that, you killed her."

That got his eyes off Ella. "Pick up that gun, Elliott."

"How about Stapert's sister?"

Grove nodded. "I never knew she was around but I always knew. I felt her eyes on me."

"You didn't know she'd been warned off by Captain Wallace?"

"That old crook? Morrie Bender owned him to the back teeth. No, I never heard he'd warned her off. I was on the outside looking in when Wallace was running things. But I felt somebody's eyes just the same.

"I thought they might be yours," Grove added, turning back to my wife.

Ella had always said that Grove was afraid of her and she'd been right. Not because she represented hearth and home, as I'd joked, but because she might have remembered him from the Sea Hawk days.

"Why did Gallimore have to die?"

"Because she wouldn't quit. Because she sent the old mick after me. Because she sent you after me, though you didn't know it was me you were after. I followed you from the Intersection. I knew you were lying about not having any leads on Maguire's murder. I knew you'd take me to whoever'd set him on me. And you did."

Mentioning the Intersection reminded Grove of the MIA bracelet that had so fascinated him at the bar. He glanced down at my wrist again for the merest second. In that second, I saw a last desperate play I could use if Sharpe didn't arrive before I ran out of questions. A damn movie trick.

"How did you get Paddy into that alley?"

"He made a mistake. He tried to get the file on the Sea Hawk murder from some old chair warmer at headquarters. Maguire didn't know I had a string tied to that file. No one could touch it without me finding out. I saw that he got the file, with a little extra included. Contact information for Little Al Alsip."

"How do you contact the bottom of a lake?"

Grove grinned wildly. "It was just an LA phone number. Belonged to a stoolie I own. He set up an appointment as Alsip. I kept it."

I finally heard sirens. Grove heard them, too.

"Time's up, Elliott. I'll get your fingerprints in a minute. You shot at me and hit your wife. Wheeler caught a stray round. That's how it'll read."

There wasn't a prayer of making the frame stick. I would have pointed that out if Grove had been present in the here and now.

"That's how it'll read," he repeated. "That's how it'll read."

"Wait," I said. "Take this for me."

I held out my left arm. When Grove's eyes locked on the MIA bracelet, I reached out with my right hand and pulled the band free. At the same time, I located the thirty-eight with the toe of my shoe and spun it without looking down to see if I'd made things better or worse.

"Why?" Grove asked.

"Somebody's got to wear it for Billy. You said so yourself."

The play had an unexpected side effect. It woke Ella.

"Don't, Scotty."

Grove didn't seem to hear her. "Why me?"

"You were a soldier. You know what it's like to be forgotten halfway around the world. You wear it for Billy. Take it."

I made my hand shake even more than it wanted to. So much, in fact, that I dropped the bracelet.

It did its part, landing on edge and rolling, Grove's eyes following it. I stooped and grabbed the gun.

We fired at the same instant. It wasn't an easy shot for either of us. Grove was being shoved sideways by Ella, and I was wing shooting on one knee. But we both hit our targets.

CHAPTER THIRTY-FOUR

I found myself in a jumbled dream about the night I'd chased a certain jade necklace around Hollywood. I'd gotten to the part where I decked the villain of the piece, only in the dream version, I got decked but good. When I opened my eyes, 1946 and the necklace were gone, and Hodson McLean was gazing down at me. I considered it a lousy trade.

"Ah, good," he said. "You're with us again."

I could see him amending a mental list, perhaps deleting an order for flowers.

"A bullet creased your skull," he told me. "Gave you a serious concussion. Not your first, from what I'm told. You'll be off your feet for a while. Your aim was truer, by the way. You shot the other gentleman through the heart."

On cue my head began to pound. It was all I could do to keep my eyes open. "Ella?"

"Fine. A very brave woman, your wife. I was happy to meet her at last. She'll be disappointed she wasn't here when you awoke— she stayed by your side all night—but Lieutenant Sharpe requested her presence.

"I came by to see how you were doing and to congratulate you. I knew you would avenge Mr. Maguire if anyone could. We're expecting an uptick in telephone inquiries as a result of the initial news stories, with the likelihood of more business to follow."

I thought he might start citing statistics—calls per round

expended maybe—but he checked himself, and his rosy scalp grew rosier as I watched.

"You did well, Scott. I'll go and find Mrs. Elliott, shall I?"

He paused at the door. "Take all the time away you need. Your desk is clear."

That wasn't how I remembered it. "About Amos Decker—"

"That file is closed, I'm afraid. Mr. Decker overdosed in a Las Vegas hotel room yesterday. A sad, wasteful end."

So Decker would never receive his lifetime achievement award. I felt bad about that until Ella entered, looking like she'd come from nothing tougher than a set of tennis. Gabrielle appeared in the doorway and waited there.

I tried to sit up, heard "The Anvil Chorus," and slumped back down again. By then, Ella had taken my hand. Gabby slipped up behind her.

McLean the canny observer had been right about my wife. She was fine. The ghost of Sugar Stapert had been laid at last.

Ella reached for but didn't quite touch my bandaged temple. "We're here to take you home, Scotty."

"Which home?"

"Our home."

I closed my eyes. "Lead me to it," I said.

About the Author

Terence Faherty's stories about Hollywood sleuth Scott Elliott have won two Shamuses for distinguished work in the private eye field. Faherty's first novel, *Deadstick*, featuring his other series character, former seminarian Owen Keane, was nominated for an Edgar in 1991.The author's short fiction appears regularly in mystery magazines and anthologies and has won the Macavity Award from Mystery Readers International; his work has been published in the United Kingdom, Japan, Italy, and Germany. Fans of the Scott Elliott stories have come to recognize Faherty's vivid and accurate depiction of Hollywood in the years after World War II. Not surprisingly, when he isn't writing fiction he can often be found lecturing on the films of Basil Rathbone. He lives with his wife, Jan, in Indianapolis.

CPSIA information can be obtained
at www.ICGtesting.com
Printed in the USA
LVHW091732011118
595633LV00002B/277/P

9 781732 418400